FROM BEGINNING TO END

–

A NEW WINDMILL BOOK OF SHORT STORIES

EDITED BY MIKE ROYSTON

D1745528

Heinemann
New Windmills

Published by Heinemann Educational Publishers
Halley Court, Jordan Hill, Oxford OX2 8EJ
A division of Reed Educational and Professional Publishing Ltd

OXFORD MELBOURNE AUCKLAND
JOHANNESBURG BLANTYRE GABORONE
IBADAN PORTSMOUTH (NH) USA CHICAGO

05 04 03 02 01
10 9 8 7 6 5 4 3 2 1

ISBN 0 435 12535 4

Acknowledgements
The publishers gratefully acknowledge the following for permission to reproduce copyright
material. Every effort has been made to trace copyright holders, but in some cases this has
proved impossible. The publishers would be happy to hear from any copyright holder that has
not been acknowledged.

'Voodoo' by Fredric Brown; copyright by the Estate of Fredric Brown, reprinted by permission
of the Estate and its agents, Scott Meredith Literary Agency, LP. 'A Grave Misunderstanding' by
Leon Garfield, reprinted by permission of John Johnson (Authors' Agent) Ltd, London.
'Pure Rotten' by John Lutz, first published in *Mike Shane Mystery Magazine*, August 1977;
copyright 1977 by Renown Publications Inc., reprinted by permission of the author. 'The First
Day at School' by William Saroyan, from *The Best Stories of William Saroyan*, reprinted by
permission of Laurence Pollinger Ltd on behalf of the William Saroyan Foundation and the
Stanford University Libraries. 'Sing-Song Time' by Joyce Grenfell from *George, Don't Do That,*
published by Macmillan; © Joyce Grenfell 1977, reprinted with permission of
Sheila Land Associates Ltd. 'Love Letters' by Kate Walker, from *State of the Heart* edited by P.
Matthews, published by Omnibus Books Australia 1988, reprinted by permission of the author.
'Romantic Interlude' by Timothy Callender, from *It So Happens,* published by Heinemann
Educational, reprinted by permission of REPP. 'Like Mother, Like Son' by Pauline Cartledge and
'Perhaps There's Something To Be Said For The Three Rs After All' by Nicholas Hodgson, taken
from the *Daily Telegraph,* 3rd May, 1997. © The Telegraph Group Ltd, 3rd May 1997, used with
permission. 'Saturday the Fifth' by Kate Edwards, from *Splinters,* edited by R. Baines, published
by Oxford University Press, Australia. 'The Dead Don't Steal' by Ella Griffiths, reprinted by
permission of Laurence Pollinger Ltd on behalf of the Estate of Ella Griffiths. 'Forbidden
Clothes' by Jamila Gavin, from *Mixed Feelings,* published by Mammoth, an imprint of Egmont
Children's Books Ltd, reprinted with permission of David Higham Associates Ltd. 'Rendezvous'
by Ed Gorman, first published in *Splinters* edited by R. Baines, published by Oxford University
Press, Australia, reprinted by permission of International Scripts, on behalf of the author.
'Dog on Board' by Dennis Hamley, from 'The New Oxford Book of Supernatural Stories',
reprinted by permission of the author. 'The Gulf' by Geraldine McCaughrean, first published in
Dare to be Different, by Bloomsbury, reprinted by permission of the author.

Cover photo by Stone
Cover design by Philip Parkhouse Design

Illustrations by Jackie Hill at 320 Design; 'A Grave Misunderstanding' – Neil Parker; 'Romantic
Interlude' – John Holder; 'The Dead Don't Steal' – Hashim Akib; 'Forbidden Clothes' – Hashim
Akib; 'Dog on Board' – Hashim Akib; 'The Gulf' – Hashim Akib
Typeset by TekArt, Croydon, Surrey
Printed and bound in the United Kingdom by Clays Ltd, St Ives plc

Contents

Introduction for Students

This collection illustrates some of the different **forms** and **structures** short stories can take. It invites you to ask: 'Why did the writer choose *that* way of presenting the story for *this* subject?'

The business of 'choosing' is important. Ideas for stories don't come complete with instructions on how to assemble them. The structure of a good story has to be worked at before it feels right for what it describes.

Imagine you have dreamed up the perfect murder mystery story. How do you *begin* it so your reader is still with you at the second paragraph? How can you keep the suspense going once the body's been discovered? How will you spring that surprise ending you've kept up your sleeve, without giving the game away halfway through? Unless you find really good answers, and carry them into the writing, your perfect murder mystery won't make the impact it ought to.

The writers in this collection *have* found 'really good answers' to questions like these. The way they put their stories together matches their intentions and the subjects they write about, subjects including: voodoo; a murdered woman who apparently steals cars; the pressures modern life puts on teenagers; and two kinds of blackmail.

At the back of the book are Activities to encourage you to think about how the stories are constructed and to experiment with different forms in your *own* story writing. The best way to see how stories can be shaped effectively is to write them yourself. Try it!

Mike Royston

Introduction for Teachers

Purposes

From Beginning to End has been compiled in response to teachers' requests for high-quality, mainly recent short fictions which have been tried, tested and enjoyed across Key Stage 3.

The collection demonstrates a wide range of forms, formats and narrative structures in short stories. Its main purpose is to help Key Stage 3 students appreciate how writers shape and construct their narratives to guide a reader's response. To this end, the Activities focus on ways in which structural devices at text-, paragraph- and sentence-level are used to:

- engage and hold the reader's interest
- build up suspense
- develop character and relationship
- establish voice and viewpoint
- signal genre
- achieve overall coherence.

Since these techniques are fundamental to students' development as writers, the Activities also support them in creating their *own* narratives, using the stories as writing models.

Order of stories

Broadly speaking, the stories have been sequenced so that they progress through the volume in terms of (a) reading difficulty, and (b) sophistication of form and structure. In addition, they have been arranged to facilitate theme- and genre-based comparison, as the chart on page 133 shows.

Using the collection

The chart on page 133 is designed to help teachers make flexible use of this collection. It highlights:

- the principal theme and/or genre of each story
- the main formal and structural elements of each story
- stories which invite comparison through theme and/or structure
- stories which begin and/or end in strikingly original ways.

The intention is to guide teachers to stories which meet their needs for different age- and ability-levels at Key Stage 3. For instance: two crime thrillers, *The Great Secret* and *Pure Rotten*, are readily accessible to most students in Years 7, 8 and 9. They could be used to complement an existing scheme of work on genre. Additionally, they could be compared to show how their very different use of 'twist' endings and first- and third-person voices serves to develop plot and portray character. A third crime story, *Saturday the Fifth,* might then be introduced to extend work on the structure of narrative, since it employs multiple viewpoints within a letters format.

Many other approaches are possible. *The First Day of School* and *Sing-Song Time* can be read together to show how different narrative structures are used to explore a common subject. *Like Mother, Like Son* (a mini-saga) and *A Pound of Flesh* (a collage story) will challenge students to respond to innovative forms, as well as to experiment with them in their own story writing.

Inevitably, the chart offers only a limited number of signposts. The more familiar teachers become with the stories, the more resources they will find in them to meet curriculum aims for Reading and Writing at this crucial Key Stage.

Story selection

Most of the sixteen stories are likely to be new to teachers. During trialling, the chief concern has been to identify stories which appeal in subject-matter and form to the whole of Key Stage 3, not least to boys. Classroom feedback indicates that they are highly enjoyable in their own right and provide a fresh stimulus for both analytical and creative work.

Mike Royston

Voodoo
Fredric Brown

Mr Decker's wife had just returned from a trip to Haiti – a trip she had taken alone – to give them a cooling off period before they discussed a divorce.

It hadn't worked. Neither of them had cooled off in the slightest. In fact, they were finding now they hated one another more than ever.

'Half,' said Mrs Decker firmly. 'I'll not settle for anything less than half the money plus half of the property.'

'Ridiculous!' said Mr Decker.

'Is it? I could have it all, you know. And quite easily, too. I studied voodoo while in Haiti.'

'Rot!' said Mr Decker.

'It isn't. And you should be glad that I am a good woman for I could kill you quite easily if I wished. I would then have *all* the money and *all* the real estate, and without any fear of consequences. A death accomplished by voodoo cannot be distinguished from death by heart failure.'

'Rubbish!' said Mr Decker.

'You think so? I have wax and a hatpin. Do you want to give me a tiny pinch of your hair or a fingernail clipping or two – that's all I need – and let me show you?'

'Nonsense!' said Mr Decker.

'Then why are you afraid to have me try? Since *I* know it works, I'll make you a proposition. If it doesn't kill you, I'll give you a divorce and ask for nothing. If it does, I'll get it all automatically.'

'Done!' said Mr Decker. 'Get your wax and hatpin.' He glanced at his fingernails. 'Pretty short. I'll give you a bit of hair.'

When he came back with a few short strands of hair in

the lid of an aspirin tin, Mrs Decker had already started softening the wax. She kneaded the hair into it, then shaped it into the rough effigy of a human being.

'You'll be sorry,' she said, and thrust the hatpin into the chest of the wax figure.

Mr Decker was surprised, but he was more pleased than sorry. He had not believed in voodoo, but being a cautious man he never took chances.

Besides, it had always irritated him that his wife so seldom cleaned her hairbrush.

A Grave Misunderstanding
Leon Garfield

I am a dog. I think you ought to know right away. I don't want to save it up for later, because you might begin to wonder what sort of person it was who went about on all fours, sniffing at bottoms and peeing up against lamp-posts in the public street. You wouldn't like it; and I don't suppose you'd care to have anything more to do with me.

The truth of the matter is, we have different standards, me and my colleagues, that is; not in everything, I hasten to bark, but in enough for it to be noticeable. For instance, although we are as fond of a good walk as the next person, love puppies and smoked salmon, we don't go much on reading. We find it hard to turn the pages. But, on the other paw, a good deep snoutful of mingled air as it comes humming off a rubbish dump can be as teasing to us as a sonnet. Indeed, there are rhymes in **rancid odours** such as you'd never dream of; and every puddle tells a story.

We see things, too. Only the other day, when me and my Person were out walking, and going as brisk as biscuits, through the green and quiet place of marble trees and stony, lightless lamp-posts, where people bury their bones and never dig them up, I saw a ghost. I stopped. I glared, I growled, my hair stood on end –

'What the devil's the matter with you now?' demanded my Person.

'What a beautiful dog!' said the ghost, who knew that I knew what she was, and that we both knew that my Person did not.

---

rancid odours: bad smells

She was the lifeless, meaningless shell of a young female person whose bones lay not very far away. No heartbeat within her, there was wind in her veins, and she smelled of worm-crumble and pine.

'Thank you,' said my Person, with a foolishly desiring smile: for the ghost's eyes were very come-hitherish, even though her hither was thither, under the grass. 'He *is* rather a handsome animal. Best of breed at Cruft's you know.' The way to his heart was always open through praise of me.

'Does he bite?' asked the ghost, watching me with all the empty care of nothingness trying to be something.

'SHE'S DEAD – SHE'S DEAD!'

'Stop barking!' said my Person. 'Don't be frightened. He wouldn't hurt a fly. Do you come here often?'

'Every day,' murmured the ghost, with a sly look towards her bones. She moved a little nearer to my Person. A breeze sprang up, and I could smell it blowing right through her, like frozen flowers. 'He looks very fierce,' said the ghost. 'Are you sure that he's kind?'

'COME AWAY – COME AWAY!'

'Stop barking!' commanded my Person, and looked at the ghost with springtime in his eyes. If only he could have smelled the dust inside her head, and heard the silence inside her breast! But it was no good. All he could see was a silken smile. He was only a person, and blindly trusted his eyes . . .

'Dogs,' said the ghost, 'should be kept on a lead in the churchyard. There's a notice on the gate.' She knew that I knew where she was buried, and that I'd just been going to dig up her bones.

My Person obeyed; and the ghost looked at me as if to say, 'Now you'll never be able to show him that I'm dead!'

'SHE'S COLD! SHE'S EMPTY! SHE'S GRAND-DAUGHTER DEATH!'

'Stop barking!' shouted my Person, and dragging me after, walked on, already half in love with the loveless ghost.

We passed very close to her bones. I could smell them, and I could hear the little nibblers dryly rustling. I pulled, I strained, I jerked to dig up her secret . . .

'He looks so wild!' said the ghost. 'His eyes are rolling and his jaws are dripping. Are you sure he doesn't have a fever? Don't you think he ought to go to the vet?'

'He only wants to run off and play,' said my Person. 'Do you live near here?'

'YES! YES! RIGHT BY THAT MARBLE LAMP-POST! SIX PAWS DEEP IN THE EARTH!'

'Stop barking!' said my Person. 'Do you want to wake up the dead?'

The ghost started. Then she laughed, like the wind among rotting leaves. 'I have a room nearby,' she murmured. 'A little room all to myself. It is very convenient, you know.'

'A little room all to yourself?' repeated my Person, his heart beating with eager concern. 'How lonely that must be!'

'Yes,' she said. 'Sometimes it is very lonely in my little room, even though I hear people walking and talking upstairs, over my head.'

'Then let me walk back with you,' said my Person, 'and keep you company.'

'No dogs allowed,' said the ghost. 'They would turn me out, you know.'

'Then come my way!' said my Person; and the ghost raised her imitation eyebrows in imitation surprise. 'Madam, will you walk,' sang my Person laughingly. 'Madam, will you talk, Madam, will you walk and talk with me?'

'I don't see why not,' smiled the ghost.

'BECAUSE SHE'S DEAD — DEAD — DEAD!'

'Stop barking!' said my Person. 'I will give you the keys of Heaven, I will give you the keys of my heart . . .'

'The keys of Heaven?' sighed the ghost. 'Would you really?'

'And the keys of my heart! Will you have dinner with me?'

'Are you inviting me into your home?'

'NO GHOSTS ALLOWED! SHE'LL TURN ME OUT!'

'Stop barking! Yes . . . if you'd like to!'

'Oh I would indeed – I would indeed!'

'DON'T DO IT! YOU'LL BE BRINGING DEATH INTO OUR HOME!'

'For God's sake, stop that barking! This way . . . this way . . .'

It was hopeless, hopeless! There was only one thing left for a dog to do. *She* knew what it was, of course: she could see it in my eyes. She walked on the other side of my Person, and always kept him between herself and me. I bided my time . . .

'Do you like Italian food?' asked my Person.

'Not spaghetti,' murmured the ghost. 'It reminds me of worms.'

It was then that I broke free. I jerked forward with all my strength and wrenched the lead from out of my

Person's grasp. He shouted! The ghost glared and shrank away. For a moment I stared into her eyes, and she stared into mine.

'Dogs must be kept on a lead!' whispered the ghost as I jumped. 'There's a notice on . . . on . . . on . . .'

It was like jumping through cobwebs and feathers; and when I turned, she'd vanished like a puff of air. I saw the grass shiver, and I knew she'd gone back to her bones.

'SHE WAS DEAD! SHE WAS DEAD! I TOLD YOU SO!'

My Person didn't answer. He was shaking, he was trembling; for the very first time, he couldn't believe his eyes.

'What happened? Where – where is she? Where has she gone?'

I showed him. Trailing my lead, I went to where she lay, six paws under, and began to dig.

'No! No!' he shrieked. 'For God's sake, let her lie there in peace!'

Thankfully I stopped. The earth under the grass was thick and heavy, and the going was hard. I went back to my Person. He had collapsed on a bench and was holding his head in his hands. I tried to comfort him by licking his ear.

A female person walked neatly by. She was young and smooth and shining, and smelled of coffee and cats. She was dressed in the softest of white.

'Oh, what a beautiful dog,' she said, pausing to admire me.

He stared up at her. His eyes widened; his teeth began to chatter. He could not speak.

'GO ON! GO ON! BEST OF BREED AT CRUFT'S!'

'Hush!' said the female person, reproaching me with a gentle smile. 'You'll wake up the dead!'

'Is she real?' whispered my Person, his eyes as wide and round as tins. 'Or is she a ghost? Show me, show me! Try to jump through her like you did before! Jump, jump!'

'BUT SHE'S REAL! SHE'S ALIVE!'

'Stop barking and jump!'

So I jumped. She screamed – but not in fright. She screamed with rage. My paws were still thick and filthy with churchyard mud, and, in a moment, so was her dress.

'You – you madman!' she shouted at my shame-faced Person. 'You told him to do it! You told him to jump! You're not fit to have a dog!'

'But – but – ' he cried out as she stormed away, to report him, she promised, to the churchyard authorities and the RSPCA.

'I TOLD YOU SHE WAS ALIVE! I TOLD YOU SO!'

'Stop barking!' wept my Person. 'Please!'

The Great Secret
George H. Smith

'We can't seem to put a finger on this guy at all, sir,' Detective Lieutenant Bolasky said to the District Attorney. 'We know that he's blackmailing these people, but we can't figure how or what about.'

District Attorney Waters ran a neatly manicured hand through his silvery hair and frowned at the report on his desk. 'These are big people, Bolasky. We can't let this phony crystal gazer get away with this. What can he have on them anyway? What can they possibly have in their pasts that they're willing to pay to keep quiet about?'

'That's the strangest part of the whole thing, sir. We've checked into the past of every one of the people Maraat has been working on and so far we haven't been able to find a thing they could be blackmailed for.'

'I see. Then why . . .?'

'We don't know. All we do know is that nearly all of the people he has approached have paid him off.'

'Nearly all? You mean some of them haven't?'

'Approximately twenty-five of them have kicked in with very large sums of money. Doctors, lawyers, politicians and prominent business executives. Maraat is so sure of himself that he even takes checks and we can't touch him because no one will make a complaint. They won't tell how he's doing it, in fact, they won't even admit they are being blackmailed. Whatever it is, they're scared to death of him.'

'But what about the ones who don't pay off?'

'There were five of them. They had Maraat kicked out of their offices, but within a week of his visit they all committed suicide.'

'I don't get it,' the DA said angrily. 'There must be something you and your men are missing.'

'I just wish that were true,' Bolasky said sadly. 'Well, I guess we'll have to turn him loose.'

'If you people can't get any evidence against him, we have no other choice.'

'I hate like hell to do it but we can't hold him on suspicion any longer.'

'Tell you what,' the DA said as the other man turned to leave. 'Before you do that, bring him up here. I'd like to see him and maybe I can get something out of him.'

The detective looked worried. 'He's awfully funny, Mr Waters. Are you sure you want to do this? Most of the men at headquarters prefer to stay as far away from him as possible.'

'Well, no wonder you've been unable to get anything on him. Bring him up here and I'll question him myself. I guarantee I'll find out how he's blackmailing these people.'

A short time later, two police officers escorted a small, dark man into the District Attorney's office. He seemed insignificant enough except for his eyes which glowed and sparkled strangely. These seemingly bottomless pools of mystery made the DA uneasy as Maraat took a seat opposite him. To hide his disquiet, Waters spoke loudly and **brusquely**.

'I'll come straight to the point with you, Maraat. We *know* you've been practicing blackmail, but we don't know how you're doing it. We'll find out sooner or later, of course, and you'll make it easier on yourself if you tell us all about it now.'

The man's thin lips curved in a smile. 'I'll be glad to tell you all about it, Mr Waters.'

'What? You mean you'll confess?'

---

brusquely: abruptly

'I'll tell *you* about it, Mr Waters. We don't need your **stenographer**.'

'What is all this? If you're so willing to confess, why didn't you tell them down at headquarters?' Determined not to let the man see how nervous he was becoming, Waters nodded to the stenographer to leave. He wished suddenly that he had never sent for Maraat.

'It would hardly have been worth my while, Mr District Attorney, to confess to those **non-entities**. I knew that if I waited long enough you would send for me.'

'How could you possibly know that?'

'I knew, Mr Waters, I knew.'

The man must be lying, but his eyes said he wasn't. Those eyes! They were enough to drive a man mad. 'Then suppose you tell me what it was you knew about the pasts of those persons who paid you such huge sums of money.'

'I know nothing of their pasts, nothing. What I know about them, Edmond Waters, is in the future.'

'What?' Waters felt suffocated, as though he were about to choke. It was those eyes, those unblinking, unwavering, somehow truthful eyes. Could they see into the future? Into his future?

Maraat leaned back in his chair with a smile of satisfaction and dropped his eyes from the DA's face.

'So you see, Mr Waters, it was really simple. I just went to these persons and told them that I could see into the future and that I wanted money.'

'You mean that they paid you for keeping something secret that they were going to do in the future? For not telling others?'

'No, not secret from others, Mr Waters. For keeping it a secret from *them*. You see, I know when you are going

---

stenographer: office typist
non-entities: unimportant people

to die. The year, the day and the hour. But for a rather large sum of money *and* your protection . . . I won't tell you.'

The District Attorney's hand had already reached for his check book. 'How much?' he asked.

Pure Rotten
John Lutz

May 25, 7:00 a.m. Telephone call to Clark Forthcue, Forthcue Mansion, Long Island:

'Mr Forthcue, don't talk, listen. Telephone calls can be traced easy, letters can't be. This will be the only telephone call and it will be short. We have your stepdaughter Imogen, who will be referred to in typed correspondence as Pure Rotten, a name that fits a ten-year-old spoiled rich brat like this one. For more information check the old rusty mailbox in front of the deserted Garver farm at the end of Wood Road near your property. Check it tonight. Check it every night. Tell the police or anyone else besides your wife about this and the kid dies. We'll know. We mean business.'

Click.

Buzz.

Snatchers, Inc.
May 26

Dear Mr Forthcue:

Re our previous discussion on Pure Rotten: It will cost you exactly one million dollars for the return of the merchandise unharmed. We have researched and we know this is well within your capabilities. End the agony you and your wife are going through. Give us your answer by letter. We will check the Garver mailbox some time after ten tomorrow evening. Your letter had better be there.

Sincerely,

A. Snatcher

Mr Snatcher:
Do not harm Pure Rotten. I have not contacted the authorities and do not intend to do so. Mrs Forthcue and I will follow your instructions faithfully. But your researchers have made an error. I do not know if one million dollars is within my capabilities and it will take me some time to find out. Be assured that you have my complete cooperation in this matter. Of course if some harm should come to Pure Rotten, this cooperation would abruptly cease.

   Anxiously,
   Clark Forthcue

                                        Snatchers, Inc.
                                        May 27

Dear Mr Forthcue:
Come off it. We know you can come up with the million. But in the interest of that cooperation you mentioned we are willing to come down to 750,000 dollars for the return of Pure Rotten. It will be a pleasure to get this item off our hands, *one way or the other.*

   Determinedly,
   A. Snatcher

Dear Mr Snatcher:
*I write this letter in the **quietude** of my veranda, where for the first time in years it is tranquil enough for me to think clearly. so I trust I am dealing with this matter correctly. By lowering your original figure by twenty-five percent you have shown yourselves to be reasonable men, with whom an equally reasonable man might negotiate. Three quarters of a million is, as I am sure you are aware, a substantial sum of money. Even one in my position does not raise that much on short notice*

---

quietude: peacefulness

without also raising a few eyebrows and some suspicion. Might you consider a lower sum?

Reasonably,
Clark Forthcue

Snatchers, Inc.
May 29

Dear Mr Forthcue:

Pure Rotten is a perishable item and a great inconvenience to store. In fact, live explosives might be a more manageable commodity for our company to handle. In light of this we **accede** to your request for a lower figure by dropping our fee to 500,000 dollars delivered immediately. This is our final figure. It would be easier, in fact a pleasure, for us to dispose of this commodity and do business elsewhere.

Still determinedly,
A. Snatcher

This latest lowering of your company's demands is further proof that I am dealing with intelligent and realistic individuals.

*Of course my wife has been grieving greatly over the loss, however temporary, of Pure Rotten, though with the aid of new furs and jewellery she has recovered from similar griefs. When one marries a woman, as in acquiring a company, one must accept the liabilities along with the assets. With my rapidly improving nervous condition, and as my own initial grief and anxiety **subside** somewhat, I find myself at odds with my wife and of the opinion that your 500,000 dollar figure is outrageously high. Think more in terms of thousands.*

Regards,
Clark Forthcue

---

accede: agree
subside: die down

Snatchers, Inc.
May 30

Forthcue:
Ninety thousand is *it*! *Final!* By midnight tomorrow in the Garver mailbox, or Pure Rotten will be disposed of. You are keeping us in an uncomfortable position and we don't like it. We are not killers, but we can be.

A. Snatcher

Dear Mr Snatcher:

*Free after many years of the agonizing pain of my ulcer, I can think quite objectively on this matter. Though my wife demands that I pay some ransom, ninety thousand is out of the question. I suggest you dispose of the commodity under discussion as you earlier **intimated** you might. After proof of this action, twenty thousand dollars will accompany my next letter in the Garver mailbox. Since I have been honest with you and have not contacted the authorities, no one, including my wife, need know the final arrangements of our transaction.*

Cordially,
Clark Forthcue

Snatchers, Inc.
May 31

Forthcue:
Are you crazy? This is a human life. We are not killers. But you are right about one thing – no amount of money is worth more than your health. Suppose we return Pure Rotten unharmed tomorrow night? Five thousand dollars for our trouble and silence will be plenty.

A. Snatcher

---

intimated: suggested

Dear Mr Snatcher:

*After due reflection I must **unequivocally** reject your last suggestion and repeat my own suggestion that you dispose of the matter in hand in your own fashion. I see no need for further correspondence in this matter.*

Clark Forthcue

Snatchers, Inc.
June 1

Clark Forthcue:

There has been a take over of the bord of Snatchers Inc. and my too vise presidents who haven't got a choice agree with me, the new president. I have all the carbon copys of Snatchers Inc. letters to you and all your letters back to us. The law is very seveer with kidnappers and even more seveer with people who want to kill kids.

But the law is not so seveer with kids, in fact will forgive them for almost anything if it is there first ofense. If you don't want these letters given to the police you will leave 500,000 dollars tomorrow night in Garvers old mailbox. I meen it. Small bils is what we want but some fiftys and hundreds will be o.k.

Sinseerly,
Pure Rotten

---

unequivocally: absolutely

The First Day of School
William Saroyan

He was a little boy named Jim, the first and only child of Dr Louis Davy, 717 Mattei Building, and it was his first day at school. His father was French, a small heavy-set man of forty whose boyhood had been full of poverty and unhappiness and ambition. His mother was dead: she died when Jim was born, and the only woman he knew intimately was Amy, the Swedish housekeeper.

It was Amy who dressed him in his Sunday clothes and took him to school. Jim liked Amy, but he didn't like her for taking him to school. He told her so. All the way to school, he told her so.

I don't like you, he said.

I don't like you any more.

I like *you,* the housekeeper said.

Then why are you taking me to school? he said.

He had taken walks with Amy before, once all the way to the Court House Park for the Sunday afternoon band concert, but this walk to school was different.

What for? he said.

Everybody must go to school, the housekeeper said.

Did you go to school? he said.

No, said Amy.

Then why do I have to go? he said.

You will like it, said the housekeeper.

He walked on with her in silence, holding her hand.
I don't like you, he said. I don't like you any more.

I like you, said Amy.

Then why are you taking me to school? he said again.
Why?

The housekeeper knew how frightened a little boy could be about going to school.

You will like it, she said. I think you will sing songs and play games.

I don't want to, he said.

I will come and get you every afternoon, she said.

I don't like you, he told her again.

She felt very unhappy about the little boy going to school, but she knew that he would have to go.

The school building was very ugly to her and to the boy. She didn't like the way it made her feel, and going up the steps with him she wished he didn't have to go to school. The halls and rooms scared her, and him, and the smell of the place too. And he didn't like Mr Barber, the principal.

Amy despised Mr Barber.

What is the name of your son? Mr Barber said.

This is Dr Louis Davy's son, said Amy. His name is Jim. I am Dr Davy's housekeeper.

James? said Mr Barber.

Not James, said Amy, just Jim.

All right, said Mr Barber. Any middle name?

No, said Amy. He is too small for a middle name. Just Jim Davy.

All right, said Mr Barber. We'll try him out in the first grade. If he doesn't get along all right we'll try him out in the kindergarten.

Dr Davy said to start him in the first grade, said Amy. Not kindergarten.

All right, said Mr Barber.

The housekeeper knew how frightened the little boy was, sitting on the chair, and she tried to let him know how much she loved him and how sorry she was about everything. She wanted to say something fine to him about everything, but she couldn't say anything, and she was very proud of the nice way he got down from the chair and stood beside Mr Barber, waiting to go to a classroom.

On the way home she was so proud of him she began to cry.

Miss Binney, the teacher of the first grade, was an old lady who was all dried out. The room was full of little boys and girls. School smelled strange and sad. He sat at a desk and listened carefully.

He heard some of the names: *Charles*, *Ernest*, *Alvin*, *Norman*, *Betty*, *Hannah*, *Juliet*, *Viola*, *Polly*.

He listened carefully and heard Miss Binney say, Hannah Winter, what *are* you chewing? And he saw Hannah Winter blush. He liked Hannah Winter right from the beginning.

Gum, said Hannah.

Put it in the waste-basket, said Miss Binney.

He saw the little girl walk to the front of the class, take the gum from her mouth, and drop it into the waste-basket.

And he heard Miss Binney say, Ernest Gaskin, what are *you* chewing?

Gum, said Ernest Gaskin.

And he liked Ernest Gaskin too.

They met in the schoolyard, and Ernest taught him a few jokes.

Amy was in the hall when school ended. She was sullen and angry at everybody until she saw the little boy. She was amazed that he wasn't changed, that he wasn't hurt, or perhaps utterly unalive, murdered. The school and everything about it frightened her very much. She took his hand and walked out of the building with him, feeling angry and proud.

Jim said, What comes after twenty-nine?

Thirty, said Amy.

Your face is dirty, he said.

His father was very quiet at the supper table.

What comes after twenty-nine? the boy said.

Thirty, said his father.

Your face is dirty, he said.

In the morning he asked his father for a nickel.

What do you want a nickel for? his father said.

Gum, he said.

His father gave him a nickel and on the way to school he stopped at Mrs Riley's store and bought a package of Spearmint.

Do you want a piece? he asked Amy.

Do you want to give me a piece? the housekeeper said.

Jim thought about it a moment, and then he said, Yes.

Do you like me? said the housekeeper.

I like you, said Jim. Do you like me?

Yes, said the housekeeper.

Do you like school?

Jim didn't know for sure, but he knew he liked the part about the gum. And Hannah Winter. And Ernest Gaskin.

I don't know, he said.

Do you sing, asked the housekeeper.

No, we don't sing, he said.

Do you play games? she said.

Not in the school, he said. In the yard we do.

He liked the part about gum very much.

Miss Binney said, Jim Davy, what are you *chewing*?

Ha ha ha, he thought.

Gum, he said.

He walked to the waste-paper basket and back to his seat, and Hannah Winter saw him, and Ernest Gaskin too. That was the best part of school.

It began to grow too.

Ernest Gaskin, he shouted in the schoolyard, *what* are you *chewing*?

Raw elephant meat, said Ernest Gaskin. Jim Davy, what are *you* chewing?

Jim tried to think of something funny to be chewing, but he couldn't.

Gum, he said, and Ernest Gaskin laughed louder than Jim laughed when Ernest Gaskin said raw elephant meat.

It was funny no matter what you said.

Going back to the classroom Jim saw Hannah Winter in the hall.

Hannah Winter, he said, *what in the world* are you *chewing*?

The little girl was startled. She wanted to say something nice that would honestly show how nice she felt about having Jim say her name and ask her the funny question, making fun of school, but she couldn't think of anything that nice to say because they were almost in the room and there wasn't time enough.

Tutti-frutti, she said with desperate haste.

It seemed to Jim he had never before heard such a glorious word, and he kept repeating the word to himself all day.

Tutti-frutti, he said to Amy on the way home.

Amy Larson, he said, *what, are, you, chewing*?

He told his father all about it at the supper table.

He said, Once there was a hill. On the hill there was a mill. Under the mill there was a walk. Under the walk there was a key. What is it?

I don't know, his father said. What is it?

Milwaukee, said the boy.

The housekeeper was delighted.

Mill. Walk. Key, Jim said.

Tutti-frutti.

What's that? said his father.

Gum, he said. The kind Hannah Winter chews.

Who's Hannah Winter? said his father.

She's in my room, he said.

Oh, said his father.

After supper he sat on the floor with the small red and blue and yellow top that hummed while it spinned. It was all right, he guessed. It was still very sad, but the gum part of it was very funny and the Hannah Winter part was very nice. Raw elephant meat, he thought with great inward delight.

Raw elephant meat, he said aloud to his father who was reading the evening paper. His father folded the paper and sat on the floor beside him.

The housekeeper saw them together on the floor and for some reason tears came to her eyes.

Sing-Song Time
Joyce Grenfell

Children, we've had our run around the classroom, and now it's time to start our day's work. We're going to have a sing-song together, and Miss Boulting is going to play for us, so come and settle down over here, please.

Kenny, why haven't you taken your coat off?

No, it isn't time to go home yet, Kenny! You've only just come.

Kenny, you've only been here about ten minutes. Come and sit on the floor next to Susan. You like Susan.

No, Susan, I don't think he wants to sit on your lap.

No, I thought he didn't.

Kenny! We don't want to see your tongue, thank you.

No, not even a little bit of it. Put it back, please.

All of it.

And give your jacket to Caroline, I'm sure she'll hang it up for you.

Thank you, Caroline.

Who is that whistling?

Sidney, you know we never whistle indoors. You can whistle in the garden, but we never whistle indoors.

Yes, I know you have just whistled indoors but don't do it any more.

And don't punch Jacqueline.

I'm sure she didn't say she liked you punching her, did you, Jacqueline?

Well, I don't think it's a good idea, so we won't have any more punching.

He is rather a disruptive element in our midst, Miss Boulting, but he does try to belong more than he used to, so we are encouraged, bless his heart.

Let's be *kind* to each other today, shall we? We are going to learn some more of the Drum Marching Song we began yesterday.

Who remembers how it starts?

No, David, it doesn't begin 'Twinkle, Twinkle Little Star'. That's another song.

Yes, I know you know it, but we aren't going to sing it now.

No. Not today.

And not tomorrow.

I don't know when.

We are going to sing our Drum Marching Song now.

Edgar and Neville, why are you standing on those chairs?

You can see into the fish tank perfectly well from the floor. Get down, please.

No, Neville, you can't hold a fish in your hand.

Because fishes don't like being held in people's hands. They don't like coming out of water, you see. Their home is in the water.

Well they do have to come out of the water when we eat them, but these aren't *eating* fishes. These are *friend* fishes. It's Phyllis and Fred. We wouldn't want to eat Phyllis and Fred.

No, Sidney, you wouldn't.

I don't think they'd be better than sausages.

Come back, please. You don't have to go and see Phyllis and Fred. You know them perfectly well.

I don't know what they are doing behind the weeds, Sidney. Just having a nice friendly game, I expect.

Neville, you tell us how the Drum Marching Song begins. Yes! That's right.

'Rum tum tum, says the big bass drum.' Well remembered, Neville.

When we know the song well we're going to march to the Drum Song. But today we'll just stand and sing it; so, everybody *ready*?

'Rum tum tum, says the big bass drum.'

Just a minute, Miss Boulting.

Where is your drum, Kenny? No, not on your head. It's in front, isn't it, on a make-believe string round your neck.

Sidney, I heard what you said. You know it isn't 'Rum tum tummy'.

It may be funnier, but it isn't right.

Yes, it is a funny joke. Let's get the laughter over, please. Finished?

Now then. Ready?

Thank you, Miss Boulting.

'Rum tum tummy . . .'

Yes, I made a mistake. It was silly, of me, wasn't it? Yes, very silly.

Sh – sh –. It wasn't as silly as all that.

I think we'll go on to the next bit perhaps . . .

Miss Boulting . . .

'Rooti-toot-toot, says the . . .'

Who says 'Rooti-toot-toot', David?

No, David, not 'Twinkle Twinkle'.

Yes, Lavinia, the '*cheerful* flute'.

And what is a flute?

No, Dicky, it isn't an orange.

It isn't a banana.

It isn't an apple.

It isn't FRUIT, it's FLUTE.

FLUTE.

And what is a flute?

Yes, Lavinia, it's in a band. It's a musical instrument in a band. And how do we play it?

No, we don't kick it and bash it about, Sidney.

Now think.

We *blow* it.

Yes, Edgar, we *blow* it, and the music comes out of it. It's a musical instrument, and we *blow* down it.

Rachel, don't blow at Timmy.

And Timmy, don't blow back.

I'm sorry she blew you a very wet one. But don't blow a wet one back.

Now use your hankies, and wipe each other down, both of you. I'm sure you're both sorry.

No, Kenny, it isn't time to go home yet.

Shirleen, why are you taking your skirt off?

I'm sure Mummy wants you to keep it nice and clean, but you won't get it dirty from singing, you know.

Yes, it is very pretty.

Yes, and it's got little doggies all over it. Little blue and little pink doggies. Put it on again, please. Yes, your panties are pretty; *and* your vest.

But pull down your skirt now.

George. Remember what I asked you not to do? Well, then . . .

'Rooti-toot-toot, says the cheerful flute.'

Rest.

Sidney, you're whistling again. And if you are going to whistle you must learn to do it properly. You don't just draw in your breath like that, you have to blow in and out.

It's no good saying you bet I can't whistle, because I can. I've been able to whistle for a very long time, but I'm not going to do it now. But I can.

I don't know why I compete with him, Miss Boulting. I really shouldn't.

Let's start our Drum Marching Song from the very beginning, shall we?

One, two . . .

What did you say, Miss Boulting?

Already! So it is. Oh, good. And here is Mrs Western with our milk and biscuits.

Get into a nice straight line by the trolley, please.

No, Kenny, it isn't time to go home yet. There is still an hour and a half to go . . .

Love Letters
Kate Walker

My name's Nick and my chick's name is Fleur. And she has a friend called Helen who's got a boyfriend named Clive. Now this Clive is really weird. Well, he does one weird thing I know of anyway: he writes three-page letters to his girlfriend, Helen, *every* day.

'What's wrong with the nerd?' I asked Fleur. She'd spent a whole lunch time telling me about him.

'There's nothing *wrong* with him,' she said. 'You're so unromantic, Nick.'

'Of course I'm not unromantic!' I said, and I offered her a lick of my ice cream to prove it. She groaned and pulled her PE bag over her head. She didn't want to talk to me any more.

When girls go quiet, that's a bad sign!

'What's wrong?' I asked her.

'You don't love me,' she said.

'Of course I love you,' I told her. I offered her my whole ice cream. She wouldn't take it.

'You don't love me *enough*,' she said.

'How much is *enough*?'

How much ice cream did it take?

'You don't write *me* letters like Clive does to Helen,' she said.

'I don't need to, I see you every day in Computers,' I said. '*And* Chemistry.'

'Clive sees Helen every day in Biology, and Textiles, and Home Science, and assembly, and roll call,' she said, 'and he writes letters to *her*!'

I knew what was happening here: my girlfriend was cooling on me.

'OK,' I said, 'I'll write you a letter.'

'Aw, Nick!' She whipped her PE bag off her head.

I was glad I'd weakened. Fleur is really gorgeous. I couldn't risk losing her for the sake of a few lines scrawled on a piece of paper. I'm the envy of the boys' locker room, having her for a girlfriend.

I sat down that night and began my first letter: *'Dear Fleur . . .'* Then I stared at the page for the next half hour. What do you write in letters to someone you see every day? I chewed my pencil; I chewed my nails. Then, in desperation, I finally asked Mum.

'Write about the things you have in common,' Mum said, so I wrote the following: ***Wasn't that computer class on Tuesday a ROAR? The best bit was when Brando tilted the computer to show us the little button underneath and the monitor fell off.'***

I wrote about the Chemistry class too, though it wasn't quite as interesting. Not a single kid muffed their experiment and blew their eyebrows off. But then I got really creative at the end of the letter and added a postscript written in Basic.

I got the letter back next day with 'five-and-a-half out of twenty' marked on the bottom.

'What was wrong with it?' I asked Fleur.

'You made a lot of spelling mistakes for one thing,' she said.

'I was being *myself*!' I told her.

'I didn't notice,' she said. 'You didn't say anything *personal* in it!'

Is that what she wanted, a *personal* letter?

I thought it over for five minutes. There were guys all round the lunch area just waiting to take my place and share their chocolate milk with the fabulous Fleur. If revealing a few personal secrets was what it took to keep her, I could do it.

'Dear Fleur . . .' I began the second letter that night,

'This is not something I'd tell everyone, but I use a deodorant. Only on sports day or in really hot weather of course.'

No, that was too personal. I ripped up the page and started again. *'Dear Fleur, Guess what? Mrs Hessel blew me up in History today for no reason at all. I was embarrassed to death. Goggle-eyes Gilda laughed her stupid head off.'*

Actually, once I'd got started I found the personal stuff not that hard to write. I told Fleur what mark I'd *really* got in the English half-yearlies. Then I told her about a movie I'd seen where this pioneering farming guy loses his plough horse, then loses his wife, then his children and then his cows get hoof rot. But even though he sits down and bawls his eyes out about it, in the end he walks off into the sunset, a stronger man.

'I'd like to suffer a great personal loss like that,' I told Fleur in the letter, *'and walk away stronger and nobler for it.'* Her sole comment on letter number two was: 'You didn't say anything in it about *me.'* And she went off to eat lunch with Helen.

It was time to hit the panic button. Fleur was 'drifting'. I stuffed my sandwiches back in my bag and went looking for Clive. I bailed him up under the stairwell.

'OK, what do you put in your letters to Helen?' I asked him.

Clive turned out to be a decent kid. He not only told me, he gave me a photocopy of the latest letter he was writing to Helen.

You should have seen it!

'Darling Helen, Your hair is like gold. Your eyes remind me of twilight reflected on Throsby Creek. Your ear lobes are . . . Your eyelashes are . . . ' And so on. It was what you'd call a poetic autopsy.

And as if that wasn't bad enough, he then got into the declarations of love:

'*You're special to me because ... I yearn for you in History because ... I can't eat noodles without thinking of you because ...*'

'Do girls really go for this sort of thing?' I asked him.

'Helen does,' he said. 'She'd drop me tomorrow if I stopped writing her letters. It's the price you pay if you want to keep your girlfriend.'

So I began my third letter, with Clive's photocopy propped up in front of me as a guide.

'*Dear Fleur, Your hair is like* . . .' I began.

Actually, I'd always thought it was like fairy-floss, pretty from a distance but all gooey when you touched it – too much hair-spray, I suppose.

I scrapped that opening and started again.

'*Dear Fleur, Your eyes are like* . . .'

Actually, they're a bit small and squinty. I think she might need glasses but she's not letting on.

Scrub the eyes.

'*Dear Fleur, Your face is excellent overall. You look like one of those soap-opera dolls.*'

I thought I would've been able to go on for hours about her face, but having said that, it seemed to sum her up.

I moved on to the declarations: '*I love you because* . . .' I chewed my pencil again, then my fingernails. This time I couldn't ask Mum.

Why did I love Fleur? Because she was **spunky**. Because all the guys thought so too. Well, not all of them. Some of them thought she wasn't all that interesting to talk to, but I put that down to jealousy.

Still, I began to wonder, what *had* we talked about in the three weeks we'd been going together? Not much really. She'd never been interested enough in my hockey playing to ask in-depth questions about it. And, I have to

spunky: plucky

admit, I hadn't found her conversation on white ankle boots all that riveting either.

No wonder I was having so much trouble writing letters to her. We had nothing in common. I barely knew her. What were her views on nuclear disarmament? Maybe she didn't have any. Was she pro-Libyan? I didn't know.

I scrapped the letter, scrapped Clive's photocopy, and started again, this time with no trouble at all.

Dear Fleur, This writing of letters was a very good idea because it gives me the opportunity to say something important to you. I think you're a nice girl and I've enjoyed going steady with you for three weeks but I think we should call it off. Even if it's a great personal loss to both of us, I'm sure we'll walk away stronger and nobler. Yours sincerely, Nick.'

I slipped the letter to her in Computers. She didn't take it too badly, just ripped it up and fed it through the shredder. But then two days later photocopies of my *personal* letter started to circulate the school.

I didn't mind, though, because as a result of that, Goggle-eyes Gilda slipped me a note in History that said, briefly: *'I like your style, Nick. You've got depth.'* I took another look at Goggle-eyes. I didn't mind her style either. She has this terrific laugh and she's a whiz on computers.

I wrote back straight away, my own kind of letter this time – honest and to the point: *'Dear Gilda, That three-minute talk you gave on speech day about Third World Famine Relief was really excellent. I'll be eating lunch in the quad if you'd care to join me.'*

Romantic Interlude
Timothy Callender

This story from the West Indies is written in Barbados dialect.

There was a magistrate live in we village name Mayers. He and Big Joe wasn't no friends, cause almost every week Big Joe used to be haul up in front of he for some offence he do the night before. Every time the magistrate use to fine Big Joe heavy heavy.

Magistrate Mayers had a real good-lookin' daughter, and, believe it or not, she fall in love with Big Joe. He impress the girl by telling she a lot of lie about how he father own a **wash o'** property all over the island, and she fall for he. But she didn't let the father know because he could get on very ignorant at a thing like that. He know Big Joe well; and he did want a son-in-law that would help he in he declining years, not live offa him, like Big Joe would do.

Anyhow Magistrate Mayers find out about this love-thing, and he and the daughter had a big **bassa-bassa**. He tell the girl that Big Joe is a ordinary criminal what no good girl won't want to **'societ** with. And when the girl hear this, she come back to Joe and say, 'Well, it look like if nothing can't happen between we.'

When Joe hear this he say, 'But Sheila, I like you bad. I thought you did promise to stay with me till death us do part.'

She say 'Well you must be dead then, cause I parting.' And she gone long and left Joe.

---

wash o': large amount of
bassa-bassa: argument
'societ: associate, mix

Now Joe get heartbroken, and he walk about all that night drinking rum and crying. So now when he was going down an alley in the heart of the city he see these two men and he stop them and start telling them he story. He feel that he must get somebody to talk to.

Well the men wasn't interested in Joe nor the story till they hear that he got twenty-five dollars in he back-pocket. Then they start winking at one another and nodding and smiling behind Joe back.

One of them say, 'I real sorry for you, man. Come lewwe go and buy a drink for you.' And all three of them went off to a little pub, and the men give Joe rum until he was drunk as a fish. When he pass out they rob him. They thief all his money and they drag him out in the alley and carry away his clothes too. And when after a coupla hours Joe wake up he find heself down there in that dark cold alley naked as he born.

'Oh lord!' he say. 'But looka this trouble, yes! What I going do now? I can't walk through the streets like this!' He really in trouble, cause he ain't got so much as a kerchief on, and he live real far from there. If the police ketch him they going lock he up and throw 'way the key, because they very strict 'bout indecent exposure around this place.

So Joe sitting down there in the alley shivering and don't know what to do. And he saying to heself 'I very sorry that I ever meet them two men. It only show you got to be careful when you mek friends with people what can happen.'

Then he was in luck, 'cause sudden so – all o' the street lamps went out one time, and he remember he had a friend living somewhere near there in a apartment room, and he decide to go to this fellow and see if he can't borrow a pants to wear home.

So he get up and walk down the alley in he birthday suit. The night dark dark dark with all the street lamps out, and Joe can hardly see two feet in front o' he; but he still glad 'cause it mean that he got a chance now for nobody to see he.

At last he reach the place where his friend living. They was repairing the building and it had a lot o' iron pipes making scaffolding outside this place. So as he didn't want to risk going to the front door in case anybody see him, he start climbing up the network deciding it would be safer to call at he friend window.

Well, he climb up the scaffolding, and just as he reach the window he thought was the right one . . . hey . . . all the street lamp lights come on again. So he dive through the window quick and start calling 'Cossie, Cossie, don't frighten. Is me!'

But it turn out he had land up in a young woman room, and when the young woman, who was asleep in bed, wake up and turn on she light, she see this big naked man in she room and she start one bawling.

So Joe jump back through the window and start climbing down as fast as he could. But by this time people appearing like ants out of the ground. And he in more trouble now, 'cause it starting to drizzle and a cold wind blowing, and he had a fresh cold too besides. And what was worse he see like a couple o' policemens down there too.

By this time the young woman had come downstairs and she holler: 'Looka the thief up there. He disguise as a naked man.'

So the police order Joe to come down, but Joe stop right where he was and won't move.

One man in the crowd then say:

'Oh, you **playin'** you ain't moving? All right, I going get you down.' And he pelt up a big rock and catch Joe right in he head. Sudden so is like if the sky come down, because Joe seeing a lot of bright stars twinkling in front

---

playin': pretending

of his eyes. And Joe get vex because he ain't accustom to people hitting him with big rock like that just because he won't come down. He climb down fast so and grabble the man that hit him, and is a fight that start. Joe wrestling like a champion, putting on a Japanese toe-hold and a Russian neck-twist and a Egyptian wrist-lock and a good old **Bajan jook** in the eye. And the man holler 'Hey, look, **wunna** better gimme a hand with this man, he like he wanta give trouble.'

So everybody hold onto Joe and they tie him up and put he in the van, and the police slam the door and get in and drive away to the police station with Big Joe.

And the next morning they haul Big Joe up before Magistrate Mayers, and Mayers was cruel that day, especially since he now know that Joe had eyes on he daughter. I don't say he was prejudice, but he start calling Joe a vagabond and a undesirable element from the time he step in the court.

Joe appealing to him and sayin' how he is a poor man and that he sick, he like he catch pneumonia last night out there naked in the cold, and that he got a old mother to support.

And the magistrate say 'You ketch pneumonia last night, and you going ketch hell in here to-day, I telling you.'

This get Joe blood hot, and he start climbing up to get at the magistrate, and when Mr Mayers see him looking so cruel, like he change his mind and say 'Stop! Stop! Like you really looking sick. I going to give you a chance this time, young man. You is convicted, reprimanded, and discharged.'

So Joe walk out o' the court a free man, and, since Mr Mayers had deal so lenient with he, a few days later he gone to the man home to ax him for he daughter's hand.

Bajan jook: Barbadian fist
wunna: you

He really didn't expect to get the father's foot. Anyway Joe let this pass 'causin' the girl looking on and still ain't tekking no notice of him.

Well, Joe start one big pining 'way. At last he say to heself 'My life ain't worth living no more. The onliest thing to do is to commit 'sassination.'

So he run down in the gully whereside the big pond is intending was to drown heself. He fill up all he pockets with big rocks to keep he under the water, and when he get to the edge o' the pond, he tek a header and went over.

But he did forget that it did the dry season and that all the pond had dry up, so instead o' landing in the water he come down – buddung – 'pon the pond-bottom and spatter out 'pon he face.

After two days he wake up and find heself in a hospital bed, with bandages all over he body. But Joe was happy when he see who it was who was tending to him. It was the magistrate daughter, cause she had gone on as a nurse at the said-name horspital.

You ain' know, that in a few days everything went back lovey-dovey again between the two of them? And she confess to Joe that she like he, but is she father brekking them up.

So Joe then out and suggest that they can run 'way and get married. 'I can get all the license and paper and thing, if you willing,' Joe say.

'If you really love me like all that, I willing,' she say.

Well, after a month Joe get better and went home. The very evening he come home, he fix up he old motor-cycle and had it running good, for the plan was to go for the girl that night and both of them would get on 'pon the cycle and ride 'way and get married the next day.

That night Big Joe went down by the magistrate house 'pon the motor-cycle. Sheila come out and tell him, 'I ready. I left a note for Daddy when he come home. Come lewwe go!'

Is only because she love Joe that she get on that cycle with he. Joe does ride like if hell and high water after he. The night dark dark dark dark and the road wet and the motor-cycle skidding so bad is like they going sideways more than straight.

Then Sheila say, 'Careful, Joe. Look at them two head-lights in front of we. Watch youself.'

Joe say, 'Okay, bird, I see them head-lights. Is all right, I can navigate this machine pretty.' And he increasing speed, and heading straight for the approaching lights at 'bout eighty miles.

It had a big crash, BRAGADAM, and Joe and Sheila fly off and land in the road. When they wake up they laying down side by side in the same hospital and all two have broken foot.

Sheila say, 'Joe, what happen? Why you went and crash into the motor-car though I warn you that the two headlights was approaching?'

'Car? What car?' Joe say. 'I didn't know it was a car headlights. I thought it was two motor-cycles and I was trying to ride in between them.'

And while they was talking, the orderlies bring in a stretcher and who 'pon it but the magistrate, Sheila father. He look 'round and see them and say, 'What wunna doing here? I thought wunna was getting married!'

'How *you* get in here?' Sheila ask. And Mayers look embarrassed at the question. Then he tell his story.

It turn out that he come home and see the note that Sheila left for him. When he realise that Sheila married Joe and that he will have Joe as he son-in-law, he decide it is better to hang heself. He get a rope and climb up a mango tree in the backyard, and he tie the rope to a branch and mek a slippery noose and put it 'round he neck and everything, and then he jump off. But being as he never try to hang heself before, the slippery noose he mak in the rope wasn't slippery enough, and when he jump off, the noose didn't slip and he head went through and he fall down said way like a ripe mango and would have splatter 'pon the ground, 'cept that he come down – bram – 'pon he two feet, and they both get brek.

When he done telling this story, Joe say 'Well now, we all three closer together than ever before, causin' we all three got broken foot, and, as you is a magistrate, I want you to married me and Sheila right here and now in this horspital. I got the license here and everything, and the nurses can be witnesses.'

And Sheila father say 'You think I is a idiot? You think I would let my daughter . . .'

But when he see Joe hand creeping round to he back

pocket, he say 'He-he-he, You know I only **mekking sport**. You know I did always like you, and I sure you will mek a good son-in-law. Wunna has my blessing.'

So they get married there in the said-same horspital. And when they all come out, the old man had was to set them up in a nice little cottage.

And I pleased to say that the two o' them lived happily ever after till the following month . . . but that is another story.

---

mekking sport: joking, kidding

Like Mother, Like Son
Pauline Cartledge

1955
Dear Mummy,
I hate this boarding school. Food awful, prefects bully me. Please take me home.

Love, David

Dear David,
Nonsense! Chin up.

Mother

1997
Dear David,
I hate this Home. Food awful, nurses treat me like a child. Fetch me immediately.

Mother

Dear Mother,
Nonsense! Chin up.

David

Saturday the Fifth
Kate Edwards

The Hills News, 4 August

Wildlife in the Suburbs

As you probably know, Mr Rogers of Jeremiah Avenue has passed on. What a nice man he was, calling me by my first name Maxine and always asking how I was. He'd stick his head over the fence and we'd have a good chat.

Anyway a reasonably young man has moved into Mr Rogers' house, and he keeps to himself this one does. Every day at 5.30, when he comes home from work he goes down to the small wooden shed at the bottom of the garden, and, instead of hammering and sawing as any man should, well, like Mr Rogers, he brings out this big hawk or falcon on his thick glove.

And I tell you, this man's a worry. He's quite short for his age, and dresses casually, and he doesn't seem to be able to shave very well, but he brings out his hawk, as I said, and he feeds it with lumps of raw meat. The meat is tied to a string which he swings round his head like a cowboy, and with this bird flying low over my Hills Hoist fetching meat, well it's quite a worry, I tell you that.

We haven't ever seen a hawk in Jeremiah Avenue and I'm not sure a hawk belongs here either.

I suggest that something is done about this state of affairs before someone gets hurt.

M. Walker,
Jeremiah Avenue

Council Buildings,
Showground Road

To Mr Ray Jennings
16 Jeremiah Avenue
Castle Hill
10 August

Dear Sir,

It has come to our attention that you have a wild bird in your keeping.

We presume you are aware of the regulations and restrictions regarding the private housing of a hawk or any of the various diurnal birds of prey of the family Falconidae, having the characteristic curved beak, rounded wings and long tail.

Briefly, it is against the law in New South Wales for any private individual to keep such a creature in captivity on their own property.

We therefore order you to hand the bird over to the National Parks and Wildlife Service at the soonest opportunity. If you do not comply with this order within the month you will be liable for a large fine and may be subject to prosecution.

Yours faithfully,

Jason Morrison

The Hills News, 18 August

LETTERS TO THE EDITOR

A Bird on the Hand

Recently I have received a letter from the Council Offices ordering me to get rid of my prize possession, a kestrel hawk.

I have had this kestrel since it was a young bird.

I first saw the bird in Bowral towards the end of last year when I was staying on a local property. While working with horses in the paddock, I became aware of a young hawk fluttering above me. I watched it hover and then swoop down in the next field to catch a fieldmouse. One of the farm's working dogs also saw the bird, and before I knew it, had bolted over and nipped the kestrel on the tail. The kestrel made a desperate attempt to get free. I restrained the dog and tried to free the bird. It was stunned briefly, but soon became aware of my presence. It was a young female. She stared at me with pulsating eyes and started fretting hysterically. She began to dart at me ferociously, but I managed to throw my coat over her and finally catch her.

I was worried that her tail had been so badly damaged that she could not fly.

This proved to be the case, so I decided to keep her and look after her.

My wife passed away eighteen months ago, and recently I moved to Castle Hill taking the bird with me. The kestrel is now my only companion. Over the past year I have managed to train her to some extent, although this is a long process as a hawk is never completely tamed. I have studied the mediaeval practice of falconry, and have learnt how to make jesses, which are leg straps, and even a leather eye hood, or rufter, for her. She lives in a strong well-built shed in my back garden. Here she remains during the day, tethered to a block.

I would like to know how she could possibly be a danger to anyone?

Ray Jennings
Jeremiah Avenue

The Hills News, 25 August

LETTERS TO THE EDITOR

Animal Companionship

I wish to write in support of Mr Jennings. I admire him for keeping a kestrel hawk in his back garden. He has every right to keep a bird if he looks after it properly.

I had a special relationship with an animal myself several years ago. She was a little Corgi named Jessop. My husband John never understood, and became very angry when I spent summer mornings taking her down the park for a run. He thought that there were better things I could do with my time. Anyway he was jealous of the friendship I shared with Jessop. He decided that the dog was a nuisance, and had her put down.

I spent days on my own after that wishing Jessop could be with me to share the morning sun. She had been such good company, and now I miss her playful bark and her deep brown eyes.

It's amazing how animals can give you so much love and understanding when you treat them right.

Wendy Short,
Greenbank Drive

The Hills News, 28 August

LETTERS TO THE EDITOR

Shame, Mr Jennings

I think it's shocking that a man who sees himself as a civilised person is happy to keep a magnificent wild hawk in a small enclosure away from its natural habitat.

I am convinced that anyone who cares about the wildlife of this country, and the environment in which we live, will feel the same as I do.

I have a good mind to go over to Jeremiah Avenue and release that beautiful hawk from its horrible cage.

Animals and birds have done nothing to man other than to give them love, assistance and devotion, and yet people take the flora and fauna of this country for granted. Animal rights must be protected. No one deserves to be locked away in a cage all day, with no room for movement or exercise. This sort of slavery of animals must stop immediately. Mr Jennings is a cruel man and a disgrace to society, who thinks he's doing the world a favour.

The only favour you can do, Mr Jennings, is to set that bird free. Find something else to do with your spare time, because keeping a wild bird in captivity is not as innocent a pastime as you might think. There is always a penalty to be paid.

Karen Parker,
Belvedere Avenue

The Hills News, 1 September

Keep Traditions Alive

Mr Jennings is a rarity. How good it is to see a person like Mr Jennings being prepared to spend time and money exploring the skills of the ancient art of falconry.

In his letter (18 Aug) he writes that falconry dates back to mediaeval times. In fact it is a much older practice than that.

Falconry is the training of hawks to hunt wild birds or game. It is an extremely difficult skill to master. It is actually of Oriental origin, and dates back to 2000 BC, when it was practiced in China. It is also known to have taken place in Japan, India, Persia and other Asian countries as early as 600 BC. Falconry is the subject of some very early Egyptian wall paintings, so the Egyptians knew about it. The Romans were keen falconers, but the practice only came to England after the Norman Conquest in 1066.

Clearly something as old as falconry must be preserved. Too many traditions of the past have been lost or overtaken in our quick-fix materialistic society.

While I can sympathise with Ms Parker (28 Aug) about the preservation of our natural environment, I think it is also important to keep alive the skills and traditions of the past. I would like to remind her that Mr Jennings has not killed anything. Indeed, he has kept alive a kestrel which might otherwise have died.

Stephen Haley,
Excelsior Avenue

The Hills News, 8 September

Police Called to Jeremiah Avenue

At approximately 4.00 pm last Saturday, the fifth of September, the police were called to a disturbance at 16 Jeremiah Avenue that proved to be more than just a routine investigation.

They found Mr Ray Jennings, the owner of the property, slumped against the corner of his house, blood trickling down his face and congealing on his collar. There was a large lump on his forehead where he had obviously sustained a heavy blow. A closer inspection revealed a nasty gash at the back of his neck. It is assumed that this was caused by a collision with the fuse box on the side of the house, possibly when Mr Jennings was falling.

Neighbour Maxine Walker called the police when she heard fighting and screaming coming from her neighbour's backyard. 'He lives alone, you see, so I thought it was very odd. He's such a quiet man really. And the noise was terrible. I looked over the fence and there he was. He was sitting down, leaning against the house like. Then I saw the blood. I ran inside and phoned the police.'

It was while Mrs Walker was on the phone to the police station that she heard a second scream. She says it was even more terrible than the first. She dropped the phone and ran outside. It was then that the full horror of the scene became apparent.

The body of a young woman was lying half across a pathway that led to Jennings' garden shed. Her face and forearms had been severely mutilated.

'She was unrecognisable,' said Sergeant Johnson, who, with Constable Reeve, was first on the scene. 'She looked as if she had been in a fight with a piece of machinery of some sort.'

Near her body was a heavy pair of pliers.

The shed itself was a mess. A thick wire mesh had been cut across, and some wooden panels had been torn away.

'Parts of the shed looked as though someone had fired a rocket through it,' said Sergeant Johnson.

Mrs Walker was able to help the police with information. 'Ray kept a hawk in there,' she said. 'He had this kestrel bird, you know.'

The bird was nowhere to be seen.

The Dead Don't Steal
Ella Griffiths

The ringing of the phone on his desk brought Curt Lessner's head up with a jerk. Every time it rang he was afraid it was the police.

This time it was – the Traffic Division.

'Morning, Mr Lessner,' a friendly **Bergen** voice said. 'Inspector Svendsen here. We've found your car. At least, our friends **across the border** have. Found it in Arvika – double-parked outside a supermarket. Double-parked and with a lady's handbag on the seat. Full of the usual junk, you know – powder compact, comb, all that sort of stuff. Driving licence, too. *And* a couple of credit cards. Shouldn't take long to trace who owns it. One of my lads is on to it now.'

A feeble 'Oh?' was all Lessner was able to manage before the inspector went on: 'The Swedes drove your car to the border and we picked it up there. The forensic boys'll have to give it a good going-over first – prints, you know, things like that – then you can have it back. It's all in one piece, so don't worry.'

'Well, thank you,' Curt Lessner said, clearing his throat. 'Strange that someone should leave a handbag in it, though, isn't it?' he ventured.

'The woman who took your car did more than leave her bag behind,' Inspector Svendsen answered. 'On the way to Arvika she stopped at a café. Anders', it's called. Just the other side of the border. Had a snack. Well, a dinner, actually. Meat and veg and all the trimmings. Anyway, somehow she managed to break a sauceboat.

Bergen: a city in the south of Norway
across the border: i.e. in Sweden

Sauce all over the place, the manager said. Most of it went on to the sofa, I gather. Nothing on her, apparently. The manager took it in his stride, but she was awfully put out, it seems – wanted to pay for the damage and getting the sofa cleaned. In the end she left her card so that they could contact her when they knew what it came to. So there you are: we've had it handed to us on a plate, so to speak.' The inspector laughed heartily at his own joke.

'But how did you find all this out so quickly?' Lessner asked. 'That she'd stopped at a café, I mean.'

'Simple. The bill from Anders' was in her bag. Dated the same day. The Swedish police checked with the café, and there you are.'

'But if you know that much, then you must know her name as well. I mean to say, driving licence and all that . . .'

'Of course we do,' the policeman agreed. 'It's no secret. Lillen Aas. Lillen Johanne Aas, to be exact. Lives in Skippergaten, out at Nordstrand. Number twenty-two. Three-roomed flat. Very nice too, I hear. Not my department, actually, but I sent one of our cars up to have a look. There was no one home. Never mind, she's bound to turn up soon. And when she does we'll let you know.'

'Lillen Aas?' Curt Lessner stammered. 'But she's my secretary! She's been off work for a few days – since Monday, in fact. But it's only been two days since my car disappeared . . .'

'Nothing very strange about that,' said the inspector. 'She could have taken your car without showing up for work, couldn't she? Did you ever lend it to her, by the way?'

'Yes, sometimes. Odd errands for the office, you know.'

'Will you be wanting to take the matter further, Mr Lessner?' the inspector asked. 'Prosecute, that is.'

'Er, er . . . I don't know.' Lessner made an effort to pull himself together. 'I suppose I ought to, really. But Lillen . . . Do I have to decide that now?' he asked.

'No, Mr Lessner,' the inspector reassured him. 'There's plenty of time for that.'

Curt Lessner thanked him and put the phone down. His mind reeling, he buried his face in his hands. Lillen – Lill – couldn't possibly have stolen his car. Nor could she have broken a sauceboat in a café in Sweden.

People who're dead don't steal cars. They don't steal anything.

And Lillen Aas *was* dead.

He'd killed her himself.

Everything had gone so well until Lill entered his life.

Blonde, petite, with eyes of speedwell blue, one day she had walked blithely into his office to apply for the vacant post of secretary in the small charter business and travel agency he had opened barely three years earlier.

'I haven't many references, I'm afraid,' she'd said with a disarming smile. 'On the other hand I learn fast.'

She was twenty-six. A woman, but a woman who, outwardly at least, had somehow retained the naïveté of a child.

'Can you type?'

'Yes. Not all that fast, but I'm pretty accurate. I have it taped, in other words.'

' "Taped"?' he'd mused. Strange expression for a girl as young as she was to use.

Later he had come to realise that she was full of contradictions like that.

She was right about learning fast.

She did. Very fast.

Annie hadn't liked her at all – understandably. Having been married to her Curt for twenty-odd years, she soon tumbled to the fact that he was up to something. Or, rather, that *they* were. And she'd been right. Only three nights later he and his new secretary found themselves in bed together.

After that there was no going back, at least not for him.

He had misjudged her completely. Taken it for granted that she'd jump at a chance to get into the racket. Earn a small fortune and then perhaps in a few years when they'd stashed enough away, **decamp** to the Caribbean. Both of them. Settle down and enjoy life in a country where the prices were more reasonable than in Norway and where a person could bask in the sunshine all year round instead of spending half the time frozen to the marrow. The plan was simplicity itself. All she had to do was act as a courier. Take parties of tourists over, show them around, and bring them back. Only in her luggage on the return trip there was always a wad or two of brightly coloured tourist brochures of their own in Norwegian. But she never *was* asked – which was just as well, since a small space cut out in the middle of each bundle was packed tight with cocaine.

After three trips Lill had suddenly called a halt. She wanted out. She had earned enough to make her comfortable, and what was more, she had fallen for one of the pilots on the Rio run. So that was that.

'But what about me?' he'd protested, his whole world suddenly shattered.

'You? You'll be all right. You're not exactly short of money, are you? And as for you-know-what, well – you have your Annie. You are married, you know. Besides, you're twenty years older than I am, don't forget. Twenty. That's eighteen too many as far as I'm concerned.'

If only she'd not brought up the difference in their ages! Or not smiled so . . . condescendingly. Pitying, almost. She'd made him feel practically senile.

That's why he'd killed her. Not that he'd meant to.

---

decamp: move away, disappear

Before he realised it he'd lashed out at her and caught her a glancing blow behind the ear with the flat of his hand. It had sent her reeling, and as she fell her head struck the corner of his desk with a dull thud. Even now he wasn't sure whether it was he or the desk that had killed her. What he did know was that she was undeniably dead. She'd just crumpled up on the floor and lain staring up at him with sightless blue eyes until finally, unable to bear it any longer, he'd steeled himself to close them.

Aghast at what he'd done, he'd sat down for a moment to consider his next move. Strangely enough, there didn't seem to be any blood, and it was that that had encouraged him to try to get away with it. The point was: how?

Obviously he had to get the body out of his office without being seen. Now, right away. It was already getting late – which fortunately meant that it was dark.

That was probably why he'd managed it.

But *had* he managed it? It was beginning to seem unreal.

*

After the inspector's phone call he sat quietly for a while, trying to steady his nerves. Then he locked up his office and drove home in the car he'd hired in place of his own. As soon as he got in he strode across to the drinks cabinet in the living-room and poured himself a stiff measure of whisky. Gulping it down almost in one, he seated himself at the window and stared out into the night.

Before him lay the garden, but all he saw was the place where Lill's body lay, deep in some undergrowth, well off the beaten track.

'What's wrong, Curt?' his wife asked sharply, entering the room from the kitchen. 'You've been acting so strangely lately. What's got into you?'

'The police phoned,' he answered, his face averted. 'Just before I left. They've found the car. Across the border in Arvika. Lillen's handbag was on the seat. There were some other things, too . . .'

'That hussy!' his wife burst out. 'A hussy and a thief, that's what she is! It doesn't surprise me in the least. I've known it all along. Well, it'll put a stop to your fun and games, that's one good thing.'

'Don't talk like that, Annie,' her husband said thickly. 'There's never been anything between us. I've told you so before. All I've ever done is to defend her when you kept running her down. Anyway, I don't think *she* took the car. More likely someone else who wanted to hurt her for some reason.'

'There you go again, defending her! If she didn't steal the car, why hasn't she shown a sign of life? Reported her handbag missing? She's bound to have had something in it more important than a compact and a lipstick. Women always do these days. Credit cards, that kind of thing. Oh, no, this time she's gone too far! Just wait till I see her again, I'll tell her a thing or two, believe you me! She can't twist *me* round her little finger, the way she can you.'

Curt Lessner looked at his wife without answering.

Suddenly he rose to his feet and stumbled to the bathroom. He reached it just in time to be sick into the wash-basin.

He knew Lill was dead. And the dead don't steal.

Or break sauceboats.

Later that night he was taken really ill. He felt feverish and several times he found himself in the bathroom again, trying to be sick. Only now the sole result was a heaving stomach and a dry rasp in his throat.

'You can't go on like this, Curt,' his wife said. 'We shall have to get the doctor.' They were the first kind words she'd spoken to him for a long time, he reflected sadly. Ever since Lillen Aas had come into his life, in fact.

'It'll pass,' he assured her. 'I'll be all right in the morning, you'll see. I must have had something that's disagreed with me.'

His wife gave him a searching look but held her peace.

As he lay tossing and turning, unable to sleep, he realised that she too was awake. His brain was in a whirl. What on earth was he to do? He was certain that Lill was dead. But dead people didn't steal cars, he reasoned yet again. Or spill sauce on sofas . . .

Shortly before nine next morning he phoned the inspector and told him – which was true enough – that he thought the whole story of the car theft had something fishy about it. 'Why should she leave her bag on the seat?' he asked. 'And how did she come to break the sauceboat? Sounds crazy to me. Do you have a description of her? The people at the café must remember what she looked like.'

'All I know is that she was blonde and looked very young. Childlike, the manager said. But I can phone the police in Arvika and ask if they know any more, if you like,' the policeman offered.

'No, don't bother,' Curt Lessner said hastily. 'There's no

need for that. It's just that it all seems so strange to me. I mean, she only had to ask me and I'd have let her have the car anyway. She must have known that . . .'

'Just a moment,' the inspector broke in. 'Hang on a sec, will you?' Curt Lessner heard him lay the receiver aside and walk away. A minute or so later he returned and said: 'It seems that the car was full of Lillen Johanne Aas's finger prints. So there we are – it must have been her who drove it to Arvika.'

'Oh, well – yes, I see. That settles it, then doesn't it?' Curt Lessner said lamely, hurrying to replace the receiver before it fell from his hand.

While he was shaving he studied his face in the mirror. 'God,' he thought to himself, 'I look like death warmed up.' He shuddered as the grotesque aptness of the expression suddenly struck him. At breakfast he gave up after a tentative bite of toast.

'Stay at home, Curt,' his wife urged him. 'You can't go to the office in that state. It's Saturday, anyway. And I'd be a darned sight happier if you'd let the doctor have a look at you.'

'Nonsense,' her husband replied irritably. 'Of course I'm going. Place doesn't run itself, you know.'

He changed his mind, however, when he realised that Annie was going into town. If he really had been having hallucinations, he had better find out straightaway. And the only way to do that was to go back to where he had hidden Lill's body and make sure.

If only none of it had ever happened! 'Oh, God,' he thought to himself, 'let it all be in my mind!' But somehow he knew that it wasn't.

He felt he would give anything to be able to see Lill again. Just to see her – alive! She could marry anyone she liked. He'd never trouble her again. No other woman, either. He'd learned his lesson. Dear, dear Lill . . .

As soon as his wife was safely out of the house he took

the hire car and drove the same route he had taken on that fateful night with Lill's body lying crumpled up under a blanket on the back seat. Her last drive. It *must* have been.

He stopped the car at the same place as last time. Nerving himself, he opened the door and half-walked, half-ran to the thicket into which he had thrust the body.

Stumbling into the midst of it, he parted the bushes and peered into the shadows. The body was exactly where he had left it.

At that moment he heard the sound of footsteps crashing through the bushes behind him.

It was the police.

First to arrive on the scene was Inspector Svendsen, the policeman he'd spoken to on the phone. Just behind him Curt Lessner glimpsed the trim figure of a woman. The inspector introduced her: Detective Sergeant Sylvia Larsgaard.

'I realised as soon as Lill disappeared that something serious must have happened to her. She loved that flat of hers. It was almost part of her. She'd never have gone off and left it like that. She told me once that she knew something about you that could ruin you for life, only she never said what it was. As the days went by, I got to thinking about what she'd said. That's what made me take your car. I thought that if you'd killed her and I could fix it so that it seemed she was still alive – well, with a bit of luck you'd feel you had to go back and see. She had the other key, remember? I found it in her dressing-table. And – well, it worked, didn't it?'

Detective Sergeant Sylvia Larsgaard. Blonde, petite, eyes like speedwells. Four or five years older than Lill, but even so the very image of her sister.

A Pound of Flesh

Kristin Silva

I love the Munch
As I Crunch on
My lettuce leaf for Lunch
It's low in calories
So I won't put on weight
And feel the disgrace
At the bulge that I hate.

7 a.m. Another day.

I slowly open my crusted eyes, yawn, and stretch those drowsy muscles.

I then begin my **vigil**.

I sit up and touch my chest, my shoulders, my hips. I breathe a sigh of relief – I haven't expanded overnight. I caress my bones lovingly. But to touch is not enough: one must see one's beauty.

A frantic scramble to the mirror. The lifting of the crumpled cotton over my tousled hair. Yes! Yes! One . . . two . . . three . . . I can see them all, every single rib. I swivel the top half of my body to the right. Satisfaction. No folds of unsightly flesh.

A frenzied grin spreads across my face. I am an achiever, a winner. I hurry now to drag the scales from their short-lived rest. One foot tentatively placed just to see what it could be like . . . two feet. An expectant glance.

TRIUMPH!

---

vigil: night-watch; *here*, inspection

For women in particular, the world of publicity and advertising promotes that ideal of the 'glamorous' which is usually beyond the reach of the individual. The comparison of what is normal/desirable in bodily proportions shown in the entertainment and advertising industry creates unrealistic images of the ideal female physique: slender, long-legged, firm-breasted. Miracle creams, fashionable clothes and the 'right label' deodorant can at least create the impression of having one of those 'perfect' bodies.

'IF YOU'D LIKE TO HAVE A TRIM BACKSIDE BUT IT'S TAKING A BACK SEAT TO SOME OF YOUR FINE POINTS, THERE'S PLENTY YOU CAN DO.
   THE GOOD NEWS IS THAT SHIP-SHAPE BUTTOCKS ONLY RANK AS NO. 6 AS THE FEMALE FEATURE THAT FIRST CATCHES A MAN'S EYES . . . GET STARTED ON A GOOD TRIMMING PROGRAM. HERE ARE SOME TIPS':

Slim or thin is beautiful; lean is healthy. These are the advertising images portrayed in a language far more compelling to the public than words. Confronted with glossy magazines and TV shows displaying sleek models and actresses, females are constantly being reminded that they do not measure up to the popular ideal. The compelling message exhorts us to be 'slim, strong and healthy'. Every few months a new diet crops up, followed by yet another round of enthusiastic endorsements from the formerly fat.

'Morning Mum,' I cry cheerfully as I step into the kitchen.

But only two forlorn, red-rimmed eyes return my greeting – two pained, tired, tortured eyes – as she looks me up and down. (You just don't understand, Mother.)

I sip my sugar-free black coffee. I nibble at my cottage cheese and dry toast. Then, the race to the bathroom.

Two fingers.

Two minutes.

TRIUMPH!

School's a drag. All the kids ribbing me (pun) because I look like Twiggy-the-model and they don't (jealousy's a curse). How can they gorge themselves – on sausage rolls (475 calories), ice-cream, sticky lollies, chocolate bars (Mars Bars have 270 calories), thick shakes (McDonald's strawberry shakes, 995 calories each) – in the playground? HOW COULD THEY! Surely they'd be satisfied with a can of Diet Coke.

Home again.

Homework.

Home study.

Work done. I push aside my books and turn on the radio. I glance at my legs. I wish I wasn't the sort of person who bruised so easily. Must be in the genes. Black splotches everywhere –

'PUMP WEIGHTS AS BO DEREK DOES TO KEEP SHAPE. DO A VICTORIA PRINCIPAL AND RIDE A BIKE – OR HAVE A DAILY RUN LIKE ELLE MACPHERSON, THE SYDNEY MODEL WHO'S MAKING WAVES.'

Pressure on the modern woman to be thin and therefore attractive, coupled with an enormous number of book and magazine articles, is the major cause of anorexia nervosa. Half the planet is engaged in diet fads while the other half starves. Dieting has been labelled our national pastime. Attempting to lose weight is our obsession. Women in particular fall victim to the tyranny of thinness.

'EXERCISE WHILE YOU WALK, CLIMB AND SIT . . . WHATEVER YOU DO, INVEST IN A THREE-SIDED FULL–LENGTH MIRROR THAT GIVES YOU A GOOD REAR VIEW. DON'T GO OUT THE DOOR WITHOUT A GOOD HOW-DO-I-LOOK? LOOK.

Our stated ideal? According to 'Weight Watchers', it is to look good in jeans – preferably tight jeans:

'TO BEAUTIFY YOUR BUTTOCKS, SMOOTH ON THIS RECIPE FROM ONE OF EUROPE'S MOST FAMOUS REJUVENATION SPAS . . . YOU CAN ALSO USE IT AS A FACIAL LUBRICANT:
    3 TBLSPNS AVOCADO, 1 CAPSULE VITAMIN E . . .'

The look is skinny, waif-like girls, à la Twiggy or Nastassja Kinski. And how many times are we told by the fashion pages to lose weight for summer in order to set foot on a beach and wear the minimum to the maximum!

where my knees hit, where my shins knock the tables, where my hips rub against my schoolbag.

Dinner Time.

Daddy's home.

'Come down, darling.'

Chicken and veggies. Good. (You're learning, Mother – slowly but surely.) Red meat is fattening. Never touch lamb! No potatoes for me, Mum – they're carbohydrates. They turn to sugar in the blood, then fat on the body. No, just water to drink. No gravy tonight, thanks.

An exchange of glances between Mother and Father. Sighs and sorrowful shakes of their heads.

Twenty minutes spent picking at Brussels sprouts. No one else left at the table. Bored with my chicken leg. 'Here, boy,' I call to my ever-faithful dog, Chum.

Chicken's finished. Veggies gone.

I leave the table.

Up to my room.

Have to burn off those calories. Half an hour with Jane Fonda. Half an hour with Richard Simmons. 'You can do it, girls. Come on, work it, work it. Lift those toushies off the ground!' Then on with the Dunlops. 'I'm going for a jog, OK?'

'LAST BUT NOT LEAST, FORGET FATTENING FOOD. "CALORIES YOU DON'T NEED WILL WIDEN A WOMAN'S BOTTOM FASTER THAN ANY OTHER PART OF HER BODY WITH THE EXCEPTION OF THE HIPS AND THIGHS," WARNS JAMIE LEE CURTIS, WHO HAS THE TRIMMEST REAR IN HOLLYWOOD.'

The condition is becoming increasingly common and increasingly complex. One in every hundred women is anorexic; there are over 79,000 female sufferers in Australia alone.

Anorexia nervosa is a product of our society, the extreme backlash of our thin-is-good propaganda.

And it looks like becoming the epidemic of our near future. There's no getting away from it, unless you don't watch TV, listen to the radio or read magazines. Do any of these and you'll quickly get the message . . . IT'S IN TO BE THIN.

Stupid.

Mistake.

EXPLOSION.

'No! It's not OK!' cries Frustrated Father, in full fury. 'Look at yourself! Look at what you're doing to this family! Look at your mother! Go on, LOOK!'

(Ho-Hum). Not again.

I'm sick of it.

Why can't they let me be?

I'm happy, aren't I?

I'm successful, aren't I?

I'm doing well at school.

I can't help it if my friends don't like me any more – they've changed.

What more can people want from me? A pound of flesh, maybe (snigger).

'Look at *ME*!' (My turn.) 'I'm doing this because this is what *I* want. For the first time in years, I like *me*. I'm doing it for me. *Me, me, me!*

Exhausted.

Drained.

Darkness.

Spinning.

Noises.

Voices?

. . . A blur fuzzy at the edges. Focusing.

A metal cabinet.

        Four white walls.

                Creaking bed.

White sheets, smell of antiseptic, a tube, a bottle – connected to my arm. Huge black-rimmed glasses. Three pairs of eyes. A warm hand touching my arm, my cheek, and –

  'You're going to be fine . . .'

  As Mother's salty tears drip

                drip

                She kisses me life.

'I have theorised, rationalised, agonised and analysed but I have not been able to get to the heart of the matter. Insight eludes me. I have been helped, hindered, enlightened, enlarged, divorced, inspired, informed, criticised, amused, frightened, infuriated, loathed, sustained, raised up and cast down. How any mother comes to terms with all the years of illness, fear and isolation endured by her daughter with anorexia nervosa, I still do not know.'

                A. Erichsen, *The Broken Circle*

Forbidden Clothes
Jamila Gavin

'They are taking her away from us.'

Mrs Khan articulated her words in a flat, monotone voice but, as she spoke, she leaned forward and stared intensely into the eyes of her volunteer English teacher, Margot Henderson.

Margot stared back, momentarily shocked out of her boredom. This was the first English sentence Mrs Khan had put together herself after nearly six weeks of lessons.

'What do you mean?' asked Margot.

Still leaning forward, Mrs Khan spoke again. She repeated the same sentence, hammering it out with **staccato** precision.

'They are taking her away from us.'

'Who is taking who away from you?' asked Margot, looking round.

Then she met the large, dark eyes of the fifteen-year-old girl in the school photograph. It sat alone on the mantelpiece, testifying to the reverence and devotion accorded to an only child.

She wasn't beautiful. Her face had been left to fend for itself, framed only by a severe headscarf which swept her hair away out of sight. Her nose was too long and narrow, her cheekbones too angular, her mouth too broad. Yet there was something compelling about the way she looked almost defiantly into the camera, as if she was trying to say, 'Yes, this is me. There's more to me than meets the eye.'

'Nasreen.' Mrs Khan whispered her daughter's name.

'Ah, yes! Nasreen!' repeated Margot brightly.

---

staccato: sharp

'How is she getting on at school?' Margot asked her question loudly and slowly as if the woman were deaf.

Mrs Khan opened her mouth and drew in her breath sharply as she struggled to find the words.

'She . . . she . . . not . . . fine. Fine . . . ' She shrugged helplessly and slumped back in her seat, drawing her veil across her face.

Margot felt the irritation rising up in her. Mrs Khan was not her favourite pupil. She was a slow learner, and she resented the sense of dumb depression which seemed to envelop the woman, slowing down her movements and imprinting an expression of wooden despair on her face.

'Don't just say "fine", Mrs Khan. Put it in a sentence,' urged Margot with exaggerated patience. 'Nasreen is fine.'

'No!' exclaimed Mrs Khan sharply. 'Nasreen is . . . no . . . fine . . . ' she struggled desperately.

'You mean, Nasreen is *not* fine,' corrected Margot.

'Nasreen is *not* fine,' repeated Mrs Khan obediently.

'Is something wrong at school?' asked Margot.

She glanced at her watch and noted with relief that their time was up.

Mrs Khan saw the movement. She stood up, twisting the ends of her veil in her fingers.

'Yes, it is time for me to go,' said Margot, thankfully. She was really not in the mood for trying to **extricate** sufficient English out of Mrs Khan to find out what was bothering her.

'If you have a problem with Nasreen, the best thing you can do is talk to the school,' said Margot. 'Perhaps your husband can. He speaks good English, doesn't he?' Then giving her a kindly pat on the arm, she gathered up her text book.

'Try and work through the exercises we have covered

---

extricate: free, disentangle; *here*, drag, coax

today, OK? And I'll see you next week.' Then she made her own way to the front door and opened it.

'Goodbye, Mrs Khan.'

Mrs Khan didn't reply, but stood in the semi-darkness at the rear of the hall. She looked as if she were being swallowed up within her satin tunic and pyjamas, as she clutched the veil around herself.

'By-ee!' repeated Margot, giving a cheery wave, and shut the front door behind her.

'Nasreen! Nasreen! Come on, we'll miss the bus!' Louise Dibben danced impatiently at her friend's elbow, as she stood in front of the long mirror, fluffing out her hair and squirting clouds of hair lacquer into it.

'How do I look?' asked Nasreen, twisting her head to examine her profile.

'You look great, really great! Now come on. If we miss the bus it will be all for nothing.'

'OK, I'm coming.' She gave a last critical glance at herself. The transformation was pretty good. From her demure, sexless school uniform with headscarf and slacks for modesty, she had squeezed herself into a tight elasticated pair of jeans for which she had secretly saved up for weeks to buy. They flattered her figure, she thought, emphasising her long legs and narrow waist.

'Does my bum look too big?' she asked, turning sideways.

'You look great, I tell you,' insisted Louise, 'and I like your top an' all,' she added. 'You got better boobs than me, lucky thing. But hurry up.'

'We're all right for time,' said Nasreen, glancing at her watch. 'Stop panicking! We've got five minutes yet. I've got to do me eyes.'

Louise sighed and sat on her bed. 'God! If your mum and dad could see you now they'd have a blooming fit.'

'My dad would kill me,' murmured Nasreen, as she brushed the mascara on to her eyelashes.

Nasreen had taken to coming back to Louise's house most days after school. Gradually she had built up a secret wardrobe of leggies and low-cut tops, of miniskirts and T-shirts, sometimes plain and sometimes with slogans brazened across her chest.

'My forbidden clothes,' she would laugh. She felt like Cinderella transforming herself to go out and have a ball, then rushing back to change into her uniform, headscarf and dull slacks, so that when she went back home she would once more be the demure, innocent little girl her parents thought she was.

Nasreen still shuddered when she remembered the pain of those early days at Merton Close. She had never been made to feel different before. But now all people seemed to see were her differences: her different coloured skin, her different clothes, her different voice and, most of all, her different religion. She was nothing but a Paki, until Louise decided to be her friend.

Louise was brash, Louise was loud, Louise was a leader. People listened to her. She seemed so grown-up. She was the first to perm her hair and wear tight, short skirts; she was the first to have a boyfriend and sit smoking in the bus shelter with him. She had opinions, and talked back to teachers, so Nasreen was astonished when, one day, Louise marched up to her with a maths book and said, 'Hey, Nasreen! You're good at maths. Help me with this.' They began going to each other's houses, but Nasreen knew her mother didn't like Louise and thought she was a bad influence so, instead, she only went round to Louise's house.

Nasreen loved the Dibben household. It was so different from her own clean, silent, scrupulously tidy home. Here it looked as if a tornado had struck it most of the time: always buried under a rubble of toys and washing, of babies' bottles and half-chewed rusks. Yet it was a good-natured chaos, and no one minded if she and Louise slumped across the sofa watching television and munching sandwiches.

'Wanna go with me to the disco?' Louise asked her one day.

'Oh no! I couldn't!' Nasreen looked shocked at the prospect, then disappointed because she wished she could go. 'I'd never be allowed,' she said, sadly.

'Don't tell 'em, then,' snapped Louise, bold as brass.

'Anyway, I've got no clothes,' added Nasreen. 'I couldn't go like this!'

'Borrow mine,' retorted Louise. Then she shrieked excitedly. 'Hey! Let me dress you up! Please, Nasreen! Just for fun!'

So that's how it all started.

'There! OK?' She turned round to show her friend her face with her painted eyelids, stiff, blackened lashes, the hint of blusher on her cheeks and just the right shade of lipstick to tone in.

'Beautiful!' exclaimed Louise, generously. 'Now let's go!'

The two girls clattered downstairs.

An admiring whistle rang out from the kitchen. Louise's younger brother, Craig, gave a cheeky wave. 'Like your jeans, Nasreen! Sexeee!'

'Oh shut up!' squealed Nasreen, but she was pleased.

Sitting at the back of the bus, Nasreen and Louise admired each other and laughed at the world they had set out to conquer. In ten minutes they had alighted in the centre of town and made their way along to the precinct where they knew all their friends would be congregating.

'Carl's there,' Louise hissed at her friend.

'So?' exclaimed Nasreen, flushing.

'You know you want to get off with him, and he's just split up with Denise.'

'Has he?' cried Nasreen. 'Why didn't you tell me before? Oh God, how do I look?'

'I've told you. You look fabulous. If he doesn't fall for you, he's a blind dope. Oh good, there's Mark,' Louise squealed, and ran over to join her boyfriend.

The telephone rang. 'It's me . . .'

'Where are you ?' wailed Mrs Khan. 'Why weren't you on the bus?'

'Mum, I went back to Louise's house. We're doing our homework together. She's miles better at geography than me, and she's helping me,' explained Nasreen, convincingly.

'But what about tea?' asked Mrs Khan. 'I've got yours all ready here.'

'Sorry, Mum,' said Nasreen. 'Louise's mum gave me some, so I'm fine. Must go. We've got tons to get done.'

'When will you be home?' asked Mrs Khan quickly, trying to hang on to her daughter's voice.

'Well . . . ' Nasreen answered vaguely. 'I think we've got another hour or two's work, because after geography, I said I'd help Louise with her maths. I'm better at that than her, OK?'

Mrs Khan hesitated, trying desperately to assert her authority.

'Get back before your dad does, won't you?'

'Of course I will, Mum. Must go. Bye!' And the phone went dead.

'OK?' asked Carl as she came out of the phone booth.

'Yeh!' Nasreen smiled sweetly at him, and slipped her arm in his.

'Have we time to go to the Flamingo? Have a quick drink?' asked Carl. 'Louise and Mark have gone on ahead.'

'Of course!' cried Nasreen, happily. 'But I've got to be changed and on that eight o'clock bus home. Me dad gets in at nine, and I've got to make it before he does, or else there'll be hell to pay.'

Mrs Khan stood at the bay window. Although darkness had fallen, she hadn't put on the light, but had drawn aside the net curtains to gaze, invisibly, up and down the empty street outside.

A hard lump of anxiety pressed into her chest so that it hurt to breathe. She was afraid, but then she realised that she had always been afraid. Ever since Nasreen had moved up into secondary school, things had changed.

They used to walk together, side by side, friends; but then Nasreen took to going on ahead or dawdling behind her mother. Even the way she walked changed. Instead of the leisurely, shy walk, she now strode, long-legged, looking more and more like a western girl despite her headscarf and the slacks under her school uniform. On approaching the school gates she would suddenly see her friends and, tossing out the word 'goodbye' as if to no one in particular, she would disappear into the school, arms linked and immersed in the sound of gossip and laughter. She never looked back these days.

That was when the lump of misery took residence in Mrs Khan's heart.

'They are taking her away . . . taking her away . . . ' She hissed her words out in English, as if someone would hear and understand her fears.

She felt a sudden surge of anger as she remembered her English teacher.

'They? Who's they?' Mrs Khan could hear the indifferent voice as Margot Henderson asked the question.

'They? Why the Dibbens of course!' Mrs Khan answered it now to the empty room, spotlessly clean, neat and devoid of any signs of human activity – just as Mr Khan liked to have it when he came home.

The Dibbens. Mrs Khan clasped her arms tightly around her body, straitjacketing herself, as if afraid if she did not she might scream at the world: 'I'm lonely! I'm lonely! And they're taking my child away from me.'

'Nasreen?' The sound of the front door sent her scurrying to the hall. Nasreen tossed her schoolbag inside, and kicked the front door closed.

'Hi, Mum!' she said indifferently, and did not look her in the eye. 'Sorry I'm late, we had tons of homework. I'm going to my room. I'm tired and I just want to flop!'

'Nasreen!' Mrs Khan reached out and touched her daughter's cheek. She wanted to clasp her, reclaim her. 'Did you have supper?' she asked. 'I made your favourite **pakoras**. Come to the kitchen and have some.'

'No, Mum!' Nasreen refused impatiently. 'I'm not

---

pakoras: onion bhajis

hungry. I had plenty to eat at Louise's. Just let me go to my room,' and she shook herself free from her mother's grasp and rushed upstairs.

Once in her room, she hastily removed the rest of her forbidden clothes. She carefully folded them into a carrier bag and tucked it right at the back of her wardrobe.

Then she sat in front of her mirror. Had her mother noticed remnants of make-up? She leaned forward to scrutinise herself and looked into her own eyes. They were still shining with excitement.

Carl had seen her home. Carefully, of course, because it wouldn't do for any of the neighbours to see her – especially anyone from her own community. They had hidden in a bus shelter while she took off her jeans and put back her school slacks under her uniform.

'What about the headscarf?' he asked, after she had shaken her hair out and re-plaited it. But she dropped her head with embarrassment. 'Oh that doesn't matter,' she said.

Of course, it did, and when he said 'goodbye' to her at the corner – he kissed her till she felt she would faint – and hurriedly walked away, she tied on her headscarf when he was out of sight and went home slowly, giving time for her flushed cheeks to calm down.

Now, as she stared at her reflection, she felt guilty. She didn't like feeling guilty; it made her angry. She didn't want to think about the shock and disappointment her father would feel if he knew what she was doing; she didn't want to think of how she was hurting her mother. At the moment, it was her mother, above all, who made her angry. She was so pliable, so pathetically vulnerable; her whole life was devoted to serving. Serving her husband; serving her daughter. Nothing she did was for her own benefit. She allowed herself to be a victim.

'I won't be like that! I won't, I won't!' Nasreen swore to herself.

Suddenly, Nasreen heard the front door. She heard her mother's puzzled footsteps hurry into the hall.

'Nasreen! Nasreen!' It was her father's voice, rough with anger.

'Nasreen's up in her room,' she heard her mother say nervously. 'You're back early. Is everything all right?'

He ignored her and called again. 'Nasreen! Get down here! I wish to speak to you.' Fiercely he switched on all the lights.

Nasreen slowly descended the stairs, pausing halfway down, her pale face looming over the bannister.

'Hi, Dad!' She tried to sound unconcerned.

'Get down here.' He prodded his finger into the air space before him.

She continued her descent, meeting her mother's puzzled eyes at the bottom. Then she faced her father.

'Here!' he prodded the air in front of him.

'Nasreen!' Mrs Khan touched her daughter's arm. She had never seen Mr Khan look so angry. Mrs Khan wanted to protect her. She clung to her arm, pulling her back.

'What is it, Rashid? What has she done? Please don't harm her!'

'Let go of her!' His voice was cold and determined. 'Nasreen has shamed me and her family and her community, and she must be made to realise what she has done.'

'How?' cried Mrs Khan. 'What has she done? Nasreen?' She turned pitifully to her daughter. 'What have you done?'

'She has been seen in the town without her veil and slacks, dressed like one of those loose English girls, wearing a tight miniskirt, high heels and made up like a prostitute. How dare you! How dare you do this to us.' He began to remove his leather belt.

'No, Rashid! No!' begged Mrs Khan. 'I'm sure Nasreen won't do this again, will you, Nasreen?'

'And it's not the first time.' Mr Khan's voice choked with emotion. 'I now hear that this has been going on for months. Everyone in the community knows about it. Everyone has been talking about it behind our backs. You have ridiculed me!'

'Nasreen!' She looked at her daughter for some sign of repentance. But to her amazement Nasreen stood before her father, upright and unflinching as he raised his arm, moved round her, and brought the belt down across her back.

'Why are you doing this, Nasreen?' the head of her school pleaded with her.'Why do you go on behaving in a way which upsets your mother and father and your whole community? All you get is a beating. Is it really worth it?'

Usually, Nasreen took her beatings and **remonstrations** sullenly, and without a word, but this time she looked up at her head teacher and said quietly, 'Sir, I'll be sixteen in two months' time. That's all the time I have left to be free. When I'm sixteen, they'll marry me off; I expect it'll be to some bloke from Pakistan who I've never met. I'm clever enough to go to university, aren't I? But I won't be allowed. I'll have to stay at home and have babies and be nothing but a good little housewife, sewing and ironing and having a meal ready in the evening. That's how it'll be when I'm sixteen. That's how it'll be for the rest of my life. Well, sir, I've got two months left, and I don't care how often I get beaten, I'm going to go into town, and dress as I like, and smoke in shop doorways, and my dad'll have to kill me before he stops me having what freedom is left.'

'Did you ever find out what that Mrs Khan meant when she said, "They are taking her away from me"?' asked the colleague.

She and Margot Henderson had met again in the precinct coffee shop.

---

remonstrations: criticisms

'Funny you should ask,' said Margot, putting down her coffee cup. 'After I last saw you, I got a message to say that Mrs Khan wanted to give up the lessons. Can't say I was disappointed. The last I heard was that the daughter, Nasreen, had run away and gone to live with her best friend.'

'What are you doing?' Louise woke and stared into the darkness. 'It's the middle of the night. Are you ill?'

She could just make out Nasreen, standing in the centre of the bedroom.

'Nasreen!' She sat up in bed and switched on her table lamp. 'What are you doing? Where are you going?'

Nasreen was fully dressed, but in her tunic, pyjamas and veil. By her side was a suitcase. She picked it up and moved towards the bedroom door.

'That's it for me now, Louise,' she said quietly. 'It's my birthday tomorrow.'

'Yeh! I know. Me and the gang, we've all got a smashing party organised for you,' cried Louise.

'Well, you'll have to have it without me,' said Nasreen. 'I'm going home. Don't try and stop me. Please – ' She put out a resisting hand, as Louise flung her legs out of bed and made to hold her back.

'Just let me go. I know what I'm doing. I've had my fun, but it had to end. I made a **pact** with myself that when I'm sixteen I return to my community. It's where I really belong. Don't make it hard for me, Louise. Please. Thank you for everything you've done for me. Thank your parents, too. I'll make it up to you one day. Promise. Meantime, just let me go without any fuss.'

Then she slipped out of the door and was gone.

It wasn't quite dawn, yet Mrs Khan woke to see a rosy

---

pact: bargain

glow through the bedroom window. She had barely slept all night long, as she had barely slept since Nasreen had left home. Now, with a dull curiosity, she slid out of bed without disturbing her sleeping husband, and went to the window.

'Rashid!' she called out uncontrollably.

He awoke instantly, alerted by the urgency in her voice. He went to her side and looked out of the window.

Nasreen had lit a bonfire. The flames shot upwards into the night sky. They could see her figure silhouetted against the firelight as from time to time she bent down and, taking a garment from the open suitcase, tossed it on the fire. Sparks flew upwards, scattering like fireflies.

When she had emptied the suitcase, she stood transfixed for a while, staring into the embers, then, pulling her veil over her head and drawing it tightly round her shoulders, she turned towards the house.

'Nasreen! Nasreen!' whispered her mother. 'At last! You have come back to us!'

Rendezvous
Daniel Ransom

PAYTON

The overcast sky causes him to snap on the Firebird's headlights.

Even before reaching the on-ramp he is travelling 60 mph.

Shoved between his legs is a cold can of Budweiser that stains the crotch of his tight tan slacks.

Drums pound from the tape deck.

His long dirty hair trails in the wind like seaweed.

The cobra tattoo on his left bicep glows with a peculiar **iridescence**.

He hits the Interstate doing 71 mph.

A VW bug makes terrified room for him.

He pulls the Bud from between his legs and raises it to his thin mouth.

He is doing 77 now, as he noses out a sports car with a smug-looking driver who has the good sense to glower but do nothing more.

The drums are louder.

KIM

From her backpack she takes a granola bar and the last quarter of an apple that is now spoiled-looking.

She huddles in a corner of an Interstate rest stop that smells woody from the logs on the roof.

She can smell the rain that is about to start.

She wishes, but only briefly, that she were back home, in her room, with her mother shouting up the stairway that dinner is ready.

---

iridescence: brightness, rainbow colours

But she needs to teach them a lesson – the lesson that at 15 she's perfectly capable of running her own life with no interference from them.

She hopes that this little surprise absence will make them more reasonable where her freedom is concerned.

She doesn't think of it as running away.

Merely proving a point.

God but it's cold.

God but it's empty out here.

Cars and trucks and vans rush by seeming important and aloof.

She wishes she were inside a warm car with a hamburger in one hand and a can of soda in the other. With some good music on the radio.

The apple tastes like hell.

She hopes her parents are scared.

They deserve to be.

PAYTON

On the horizon to the west he can see the rain start.

He supposes the farmers need it. At least that's what people always say whenever it rains in these parts.

The farmers need it.

The drums have died. A saxophone has replaced them.

Drums give him energy, a high. Saxophones make him morose.

He hits a clean 80 miles per.

Dark quick eyes checking for highway patrol cars.

He hopes the speed will stop him from thinking about the priest.

He rubs at the cobra on his arm.

He opens a fresh of Bud.

He thought the priest would be more sympathetic.

All the priest could say was you better tell the police.

He is travelling at 84 mph.

He can smell the spring grass on the wind, even at this speed.

He thought the priest should be a hell of a lot nicer than he was.

Why do you go on the Interstate, the priest had asked. You'd better call the police.

The priest wasn't even sympathetic about him sending the flowers and visiting the funeral home, which he's done three out of five times after he'd gone out on the Interstate.

The hell with the priest.

He can't do anything about it.

Nothing.

Payton wishes the saxophone would stop.

KIM

She sits inside the **john** with the lid closed trying to get warm again.

She thought public rest stops were usually busy. There hasn't been anybody along here for twenty minutes.

All cars and trucks sound far away.

The rain, however, is near. Thrumming the roof.

On her way inside she had passed a pay phone. She'd stared at it a long time, even extended a hand as if to touch it.

But no.

The game isn't over yet.

And anyway, all this misery will only make her story better when she tells her tenth grade girlfriends.

Brave Kim.

Poor Kim.

She has to move now.

Back on the macadam along the Interstate.

Get a ride before it's full dark.

God, is she going to have some good stories to tell.

---

john: toilet

PAYTON

Sometimes the cobra gets sore.

The jerk who put it on his arm was stoned at the time. At first there'd been infection.

Now, he rubs the cobra.

It's as if it needs to be fed.

The saxophone solo is over now.

The drums are back.

He feels young, strong, invincible.

To hell with the priest.

It is then that he sees the shape begin to materialize along the edge of the Interstate. Through the gloom. The rain.

Hitchhiker.

Young girl.

KIM

She watches the car pull off the road fifty yards past her.

Immediately she begins running.

She wishes she'd been able to get a glimpse of the driver.

All the other drivers she'd been able to check out before getting inside.

But it's dark and she's soaked from the rain.

For some reason she thinks of the pay phone.

Of almost lifting the receiver.

Of almost making the call.

She's at the car now.

Her slender hand on the door handle.

As she opens the door, she hears drums.

Very loud drums.

Dog on Board
Dennis Hamley

Amy was having a nightmare.

What a pity. Tomorrow morning the family was to get up early. The elderly D-registered Range Rover, Dad's latest pride and joy, stood on the drive, already loaded up. The trailer tent was hitched on behind. After a quick breakfast, they would drive off two hundred miles to the camping site by the sea in Cornwall. Amy very seldom had bad dreams. But tonight, a puzzling inferno had started up in her mind.

How had the dream started? Amy didn't know. But Mum and Dad, elder brother and sister Mark and Rebecca were in it. So was Goldie, the retriever, who licked her with his rough tongue and looked at her through deep, liquid brown eyes. She remembered this even when the details of the dream were forgotten. But now there was screeching and rending of metal, scorching heat and a wall of orange flame coming fast towards her. Mum and Dad were in front, Mark and Rebecca beside her. Their eyes were open and fixed: blood was everywhere. Goldie lay across her, heavy and warm, but also still: she knew he would never move again. She tried to move but something held her legs. And the flame came nearer and the heat got worse and worse . . .

She woke up. She was still hot. Her forehead was beaded with sweat, her nightie was drenched in it. But she was not alone. Something started licking her forehead and making it cooler.

'Goldie, I've had a nasty dream,' she said to him. She knew that if it were not so dark, his brown eyes would gaze at her softly and understandingly.

She sat up. The air struck cold on her skin as it touched

the sweat and made her shiver. There were shadows in the room which had not been there for years, since she was *very* little.

'Mummy,' she called.

The landing light went on. Mummy came in, switched on the little light which was kept just out of Amy's reach so she couldn't have it on all night, and said, 'What are you doing here, Goldie? Your place is downstairs.'

Goldie did not want to go. Mum led him away by the collar. But all the while Amy could see him, he was looking back, watching her with those deep brown eyes. When he could see her no more and Mum had let his collar go, he gave a little whimper as if to say, 'Why can we dogs never make you humans understand?' Then he trotted downstairs.

'I wanted him to stay, Mummy,' said Amy.

'He's too clever by half, that dog. Especially now he's learnt to open all the doors himself.'

She bent over Amy. 'What's the matter, love?'

'I . . . I had a bad dream.'

Mum looked at her, placed a hand on her forehead, then said, 'I won't be a minute.'

Amy heard her voice in the next room. 'I don't like the look of her. She's running with sweat. It looks like she's got a fever.'

'She'll be OK.' Dad's voice was muffled under the duvet cover. 'Let her sweat it out. I'm not delaying the start of our holiday.'

Mum came back. She carried the little thermometer and slipped it in Amy's mouth. A minute later she took it out, looked at it, said, relieved, 'Normal,' then bent over Amy again. 'Go to sleep, Amy. The bad dream's gone. Remember, we're getting up early tomorrow.'

How could she forget?

She closed her eyes. Sleep came at once – and with it, like a loaded trap waiting on her pillow, the same noise, blood, motionless bodies with sightless eyes and the approaching, searing, roaring flame . . .

Downstairs, in his basket, Goldie slept too. But now he jerked his legs and whimpered. Who could know what was going through his canine mind? Perhaps, now he had not been allowed to stay with Amy, something there was ranging far away, searching out someone else who might understand his message.

The motorway leading westward was thick with early morning fog. Now and again it lifted in deceptive clear patches, so cars and lorries delightedly increased speed. Then it would drop again, thicker than ever. If the fog could speak it would be laughing humourlessly. Some cars slowed at once, suddenly, hazard lights blinking like frightened eyes. Others had drivers who said, 'This doesn't apply to me. It will lift in a minute.' They carried on down the outside lane as if the sun shone from a clear sky.

Arthur Rowntree gripped the big steering wheel of his tanker lorry and peered forward. This, of all weathers, he hated most on the motorway. It didn't matter how careful he was: there were always idiots surrounding him. All right, his tanker was always excellently maintained. Arthur was a stickler for that. He wouldn't drive for a firm which didn't look after its vehicles properly. And this firm, Retro-Cychem PLC, positively had to. Ferrying dangerous chemicals from one end of the country to the other was no joke. Arthur didn't know the precise properties of whatever was sloshing about in the tank on the back. But he knew what he had to do if there was ever a leak – and it frightened him. He never dared think about a full-blown crash. But this morning the unthinkable had been nudging the back of his mind. He had woken in the small hours, sweating about it. He'd nearly rung the depot, said he was sick . . . But Arthur Rowntree was a rational man. Risk and danger were, after all, part of life. If a few doubtful thoughts in the morning were to stop him earning his living . . .

Even so . . .

He made up his mind. Next services, he'd stop. A mug of tea, a bacon sandwich, and wait for this lot to go.

He was driving through a clear patch now. Blue showed through the white shroud overhead: the sun would break through in the end.

Then, without warning, the fog dropped on him again, worse than ever. Hazards on, drop speed – slow enough already. Hope that the airbrakes – which even at their best had longer stopping distances than cars – wouldn't meet something stuck in front that they couldn't cope with. No, they wouldn't . . . they wouldn't . . . would they?

Without warning, he saw it. Right below his cab, impossible not to hit, smash right into, destroy completely. No hazards on, just slogging along, painfully slowly: a dark green Range Rover pulling a trailer tent. D registration.

So clearly, etched in horribly sharp detail. The black cover strapped over the tent. The loaded roof-rack. The rear window. Stickers on it. Words burned for ever on his mind.

> CHILDREN ON BOARD • DOG ON BOARD
> A DOG IS FOR LIFE NOT JUST FOR CHRISTMAS

Across the bottom of the window, white lettering on blue:

> DAN, DAN, THE OFF-ROADER MAN
> ALL MAKES OF FOUR-WHEEL DRIVE VEHICLES
> SALES AND SERVICE

The dog on board looked at him through the window. A beautiful golden retriever with deep, soulful, brown eyes. Driver and dog looked at each other: what message passed? Arthur didn't know, but he felt a well of unutterable sadness before the certain impact. For beyond the dog were three children. Beyond them . . . *And this would be their last moment on Earth. Because nothing could stop him* . . .

Despairingly, he slammed on his brakes. Even in that split second, the consequences flooded into his mind. Would what was behind him go straight into the back of his tanker? What about the appalling liquid he carried?

What if his tanker were thrown on its side, the tank breached, the contents spilled out – then the poison, the spreading death?

He found himself shouting at the top of his voice: 'I'm sorry. I'm *so* sorry. I didn't mean it.'

He kept his eyes open intently as he waited for the catastrophe.

'Amy's better,' said Mum. 'But I still don't like the look of her.'

Dad was tapping his foot impatiently. Mark and Rebecca were out, taking Goldie for one last walk before the journey. He sighed for the early hours, while the streets were still quiet and only the milkman disturbed the peace.

'I didn't want to have to wait,' he said. 'I wanted to beat the traffic around the town.'

Mum didn't tell her husband that Amy had cried and said she didn't want to go.

'I'll get the traffic reports,' said Dad and switched the radio on.

Fog on the M4. Dangerous driving conditions.

'I still want to beat the traffic,' said Dad.

Mum certainly didn't tell how Amy had cowered away when she had said, 'Come on, love, you're all right now. Get out of bed. We're off for our holiday.' The panic that was in her youngest child's eyes troubled her deeply.

The tanker lorry slid to a halt. For a moment, Arthur Rowntree sat in his cab, head bowed over the steering wheel, unable to look up. Then he forced himself.

His tanker had come to rest safely, two metres behind a stationary lorry. TRELAWNEY TRANSPORT SERVING CORNWALL was emblazoned on the back.

He jumped down from the cab and walked round the tanker. All seemed OK. Behind him was a black Ford Mondeo, headlights and hazards on.

Where was the Range Rover? He stepped on to the hard shoulder. Perhaps it had miraculously sheered off to avoid him. He could not see more than five metres either way. He leaned up against the side of his cab, relief flooded through him. His premonitions had not been fulfilled. He was safe – and so was his terrible cargo.

But what extraordinary thing had happened? He walked forward and knocked on the cab door of the lorry from Cornwall.

'What is it, m'dear?' said a west-country voice.

'Did a Range Rover and trailer go past you on the hard shoulder?'

'No.' The driver opened the door and dropped down to the ground. 'He'd be a fool if he tried. I reckon there's a mess ahead.'

So what happened to that tight, confident little family and their dog? Arthur Rowntree's mind was in turmoil. But he forced himself into listening to the Cornishman.

'How big a mess?' he said.

As if in answer came the wails of police cars and ambulances. Without warning, the fog started to clear. The chaos and carnage of wrecked cars and lorries ahead was plain to see.

'Strewth!' said the Cornishman.

They were on their way at last. Amy was happy now they had climbed into Daddy's lovely big green car they had bought from the funny man Dan, seen Goldie safe in his place at the back with the parcel shelf taken out, and knew her duty was to keep looking behind to make sure he kept there and the tent stayed hitched up.

Mum whispered to Dad. 'She says she had bad dreams about today.'

'Excitement,' said Dad. 'All kids get it.'

He switched on the radio. A news bulletin. A bad pile-up in the fog on the M4. Three killed, fifteen injured.

Long delays until it was cleared. Caused by stupid, suicidal driving.

'Amy should have some more bad dreams,' said Dad. 'If we'd left when I wanted, we could have been in that.'

Arthur Rowntree and his west-country companion stared at the scene. Ambulances drove off, police in their dozens tried to sort things out, breakdown lorries arrived.

'It'll be a fair while before we're off,' said the Cornishman.

'I don't get it,' said Arthur Rowntree. 'There was *definitely* a D-registration green Range Rover pulling a trailer tent in front of me. Golden retriever in the back. I *can't* be wrong.'

'There's no green Range Rover in that lot,' said the Cornishman, peering ahead.

'Without it, I'd have been in the back of you,' said Arthur. 'And then what?'

'Forget it,' said the Cornishman. 'It never happened.'

The fog was nearly gone: the sun gained strength. Arthur went back to his cab and brought out sandwiches and a thermos of coffee. Then he leaned up against the side of the Trelawney Transport lorry, sharing them with the Cornishman and talking companionably.

'Where are you off to, then?' said the Cornishman.

'Only Swindon. And you?'

'Nearly all the way. Not far short of Penzance. I won't get there till evening now. If this wreck makes it.'

For the first time, Arthur looked at his lorry. It was old – C registration. He knew that when it started thick black diesel fumes would choke the air.

'I keep telling Trelawney to get new lorries. "Where's the money coming from?" he says. "That doesn't mean you don't have to service them properly," I tell him. I hope I never have to stop quick going down the hill to the industrial estate I'm bound for. I tremble every time I go round it. If I had to stop quick – well, I'd be over the edge, I reckon. And I'd take anything in my way with me.'

'Why drive for him, then?' said Arthur Rowntree.

'Who else is there to work for?'

Arthur Rowntree didn't answer, but watched the work going on ahead. 'They're about clear,' he said. 'We'll be on our way soon.' But his mind was still troubled. *Where* was that green Range Rover? He saw it again in his mind, every detail sharp. And then it was replaced by another vision in his mind. His friend the Cornishman, at the wheel and going round the bend on the hill leading to his destination. The two images were not to leave him all day.

The motorway ahead was clear. The sun shone and the day's heat built up. Policemen waved on the drivers who had stopped safely behind the pile-up. The Cornishman and Arthur Rowntree prepared to get back in their cabs.

'Goodbye, m'dear,' said the Cornishman.

'Safe journey,' said Arthur Rowntree. Suddenly, he felt an almost overpowering urge. He *had* to say it. 'Don't go any further. Get that death-trap off the road.'

He struggled with himself. *I should. It's my duty*. But then . . . *It's his livelihood. What right have I? It's none of my business.*

Soon they were on their way. All day, Arthur could not get rid of the two visions: the green Range Rover and the lorry which couldn't stop going down the hill. They danced before his mind's eye, merging, parting, merging again.

And behind them both were the deep brown eyes of the dog, looking at him reproachfully – as if, in some way he could not fathom, he had let the creature down.

They took their time. They stopped twice at motorway services and picnicked in Devon.

Three miles from the camping site, they overtook an old lorry: TRELAWNEY'S TRANSPORT SERVING CORNWALL. Dad was pleased: he'd been trying to pass for miles.

Mum turned to the children. 'Soon we'll go down the hill to the sea. When we're round the bend half-way down, we'll see the camping site below us.'

'Don't look at the industrial estate on the other side,' said Dad.

The Cornishman watched the Range Rover and the trailer pass him. A memory stirred – yes, that's like what his friend driving the tanker had been talking about, even down to the notices in the rear window and the dog, looking at him with brown eyes which caught his own and made him feel unaccountably sad. Well, if it *was* the same people, they'd had a very narrow escape this morning. Funny, Arthur had talked about them like seeing a vision. And even now, in the evening sunshine, the outline of the Range Rover seemed picked out in extraordinary hardness and its dark green paintwork shone with a lustre somehow beyond the normal. Was *he* seeing a vision? Would they disappear as soon as he looked for them again?

Of course not. They'd just come here to enjoy lovely old Cornwall. He silently wished them a good holiday as they dwindled away ahead of him. They deserved it.

Yet there was something cold and dead now in the pit of his stomach. He wanted rid of it. He was nearly at journey's end and was thankful. He longed to see the depot, his load got rid of, the front door of his house and his wife waiting.

'Here's the top of the hill,' said Mum.

The sea, blue in evening sunshine, stretched far away.

'Soon round the bend,' said Dad. 'Then we'll see the camp site.'

Before they reached the bend there was a notice warning drivers of roadworks and temporary traffic lights. Just round the bend was another notice:

WHEN RED LIGHT SHOWS, STOP HERE.

The lights had only been set up that day, as the road repairs started. They turned red just as Dad reached them, so he had to stop.

Amy suddenly started crying.

'What's the matter, love?' said Mum in alarm.

'I can see my dream again,' Amy wailed.

Goldie put his paw across the back of the seat and touched her. He whimpered slightly, as if to say, 'I tried.'

At that moment, the Cornishman in his old lorry with bad brakes reached the top of the hill.

If they're ever going to fail, he thought, *it's here and now.*

His foot, resting over the brake pedal, began to push.

The Gulf
Geraldine McCaughrean

The cold, thin air in the back of his throat was like swallowing swords, but he ran until sweat burst through his skin, until the sweat dried to salt. He ran until every searchlight, floodlight and white-winking barrack window was out of sight and he was running in utter darkness. He ran until night gave way to morning, and every moment he expected to hear shouts or motors or the barking of dogs on his trail.

With sunrise he allowed his hopes to rise too, like a hot, orange ball of flame within his chest. Might he after all make good his escape? Might he reach safety, against all the odds? No one ever did, they had told him. No one ever would. But the hope kept rising in his throat until it buckled his mouth into a smile.

Then he reached the gulf.

He almost ran straight into it – a gorge of such dizzying depth that the river in the bottom was only a green thread; a canyon so wide that a horse at full gallop could not have leapt even halfway across. And its sides were sheer.

Juan fell to his knees, grazing his forehead on the bark of a dead, fallen tree, his arms over his head. Had he come this far to meet disappointment like a snake across his path? There was no way over. The gulf stretched as far as the eye could see to right and left. He could leap into it or wait at the brink for his pursuers to catch up with him. But he was done for. It was true. No one ever escaped. No one ever would.

When he raised his head, Juan saw a little girl watching him. She stood on the far side of the canyon, rubbing a twist of grass between her hands. 'Want to cross over?' she said. In the silence of the empty landscape her voice floated easily over to him. She did not have to shout. She spoke the dialect of the neighbouring country. The river gorge must be the border, then. Juan had reached the border – a stone's throw from safety. 'Is there a bridge? Anywhere? A bridge?' he called.

'No. No bridge . . . But I could fetch my sisters.' She put her fingers in her mouth and whistled shrilly. Juan gave a laugh somewhere between a bark and a sob. Much good her sisters would do him.

The girls came dawdling out from the long grass and regarded him with the same solemn brown eyes. Each was rubbing a twist of grass between her hands.

'He wants to cross over,' said the sister.

'Better tell the brothers,' they said.

Ten boys emerged from the swashing grass, carrying sickles and armfuls of grass. They sat down on the far side of the ravine, dangling their legs over the rim. Their hands began to work in that same nervous, habitual motion, rubbing the grass stems together into long tasselled cords.

'Go home,' said Juan, glancing over his shoulder. He did not want them to witness either his tears or his recapture. He had no idea how much of a lead he had gained on his pursuers. Eight hours? Nine?

'They chasing you?' called one of the boys, swatting flies.

'I thought I could reach the border. But the gulf . . . I didn't know . . .'

Their sunburned faces expressed no sympathy, no sadness at his predicament. Their small brown hands just went on twisting grass.

'I'll tell the mothers,' said the littlest boy, and ran off, his bare feet unsettling flies in clouds.

The village must have been just over the ridge, for he soon returned, towing his mother by the hand. For the first time Juan realised that the grass-twirling was not a nervous habit but a livelihood. The mothers – handsome women with shining plaits to which their babies clung – were also twirling the grass together into fibres, their big hands worn horny by the coarse stems. They contemplated Juan with large, dark-fringed eyes. 'You need help,' said one.

Juan laughed hollowly. 'I am past helping. The gulf did for me.'

The women called the children together, took their cords of grass, and began, simply by rubbing, to splice the thin lengths into thicker, longer ones. 'Fetch the grandmas and grandpas,' they told the littlest boy.

Away he went, and fetched back with him the old people of the village – mumbling, bent, bone-weary old bodies who shook their heads and clutched their old shawls round them, even though the day was hot. One old matriarch, her hat as big as a bundle of laundry, flumped down amid her skirts, and the women laid their grass-cords at her feet, as if paying homage. Her whispering palms twirled their individual cords into one long rope, with a deftness which defied belief. For a few blessed minutes Juan watched with such intent fascination that he forgot his own peril and strained to make out what magical process, what cunning craftsmanship could twist grass into rope.

Then, with a jolt of hope sharp as a kick, he realized that the rope was for him – to get him over the ravine.

What well-meaning, simple fools! Inwardly he raged with bitter laughter. Even if they succeeded in making a cable strong enough to carry the weight of a man, long enough to span the gulf, how would they get the end across to him? Impossible! So much work and for what? Around him the evening breeze sprang up, and Juan found he had sat all day by the gulf watching the children and grandparents and mothers opposite labour over the rope, which now lay coiled at the old woman's feet.

That same breeze carried on it the sound of jeep engines, of sirens, of his pursuers.

'What's the point? What's the point?' he bawled, and his voice dropped into the ravine like a rock fall.

The little girl – the one he had seen first – lifted up a coil of the immense rope to show him. It was all she could do to raise it off the ground. 'Father will help,' she said. 'He is coming soon.'

It reduced him to tears – this little mite's touching, ridiculous trust in her father. What would he prove to be, after all, but yet another pigeon-chested peasant in a straw hat, chewing betel nuts and hoping for a quiet life. A man like Juan.

The little girl's father proved, however, to be a big, energetic man – a hunter. When he arrived, his jeans and shirt dusty after a day on the plateau, he found the village assembled by the ravine, saw Juan, saw the rope, and instantly re-strung his bow. His grandmother threaded a needle with sewing thread, and stuck it through the grass rope, then gave the thread to her grandson. He tied it to his arrow and, without a word to Juan . . . fired it straight at him.

The arrow gouged up the soil between Juan's feet. With trembling fingers, he snatched the cotton, winding the loops so tight round his hand that his fingers went blue. The rope was heavy, but the sewing thread did not break. Like a great anaconda, the rope's end sagged its way across the ravine, and Juan made it fast around the log. The strongest of the villagers took hold of the other end and braced themselves.

The jeeps were visible now, bouncing over the rough terrain, the evening sun flashing on their windscreens. In the normal way of things, Juan could never have brought himself to do what he did next. But after so many people had done so much, he could hardly hesitate. Hanging like a tree sloth under the grass rope he crabbed his way over

the yawning, heart-numbing terror of the **vertiginous** drop, fixing all his thoughts on the beauty of the **hawser**, the thousand different shades of yellow and green all interwoven into one speckled cable. How could something so strong be made of such frail component parts? The seed-dust made him sneeze.

---

vertiginous: dizzying
hawser: rope

The jeeps skidded to a halt just as hands – old and young and calloused – closed in Juan's hair and round his arms and through his belt and pulled him to safety. Then the villagers dropped their end of the great rope into the ravine. It thumped against the far wall, shedding a shower of seeds.

Juan jumped to his feet and shook a defiant fist at the men on the opposite bank. In his raised hand was a single twist of grass.

Activities

Voodoo by **Fredric Brown**

1   **In pairs**, act out the interview between Mr Decker and a police officer investigating Mrs Decker's death.

Believing he has nothing to lose, Mr Decker decides to tell the whole truth. What explanations will he give? What evidence will he produce? Does he persuade the suspicious police officer to believe him?

2   **In small groups**, talk about how the writer has built up this story. Do you think its structure helps to make it effective?

Focus on:

- the story's ending: does it come as a genuine surprise?

- the way the writer creates expectations of what will happen: does he manage to keep you in suspense?

- the way the story is made up largely of *conversation*: why may the writer have chosen to do this?

- the story's title: does it give too much away?

3   **By yourself**, write a story of similar length to *Voodoo* which depends on a twist at the end. Choose your own subject.

Lead your reader 'off the scent' so that the ending is totally unexpected. You might try:

- including several red herrings

- holding back until the end some important information about one of your characters

- using conversation to allow a character (or characters) to disguise their true feelings, motives, intentions, etc.

Plan your ending first and work back from that.

4   **As a class**, listen to some of the finished stories. Say which of them really succeeds in taking you by surprise, and why.

A *Grave Misunderstanding* by **Leon Garfield**

1   **In pairs**, re-read *aloud* the first three paragraphs of this story.

How many of the **Functions of a good opening** listed below do they fulfil? Make a tick-list to show what you think.

Does the opening:	
A arouse your curiosity from the first sentence on	☐
B get the plot under way quickly	☐
C introduce the main characters, making them sound interesting	☐
D establish the *viewpoint* from which the story is being told	☐
E establish the *tone* of the story (e.g. serious, humorous, tragic, etc.)	☐
F create suspense and make you want to carry on reading?	☐

Find examples from the first three paragraphs to back up your opinions.

Then **join up with another pair**. Exchange opinions and examples. Are there any more **'Functions . . .'** you now wish to add to the list above?

2   'The humour of this story depends on the idea that dogs are more intelligent than humans.'

As a class, look closely at the *middle* section of the story. How does it bear out the comment above?

Consider, among other things, the effect on the reader of:

- the Person's conversations with the ghost and his feelings towards her

- the dog's barked remarks (e.g. 'SHE'S COLD! SHE'S EMPTY! SHE'S GRAND-DAUGHTER DEATH!')

- the way the ghost finally disappears.

After reading this section, did you start to lose interest in the story, or did it succeed in keeping you reading? Did the writer give away any clues about the ending?

3 **By yourself**, write an alternative ending to this story. Start from the sentence on page 7, 'Trailing my lead, I went to where she lay, six paws under, and began to dig.'

Remember you are writing as if you are the dog. If you wish, introduce new characters. The plot can take any direction you choose, *as long as it holds the reader's interest to the very last sentence*.

4 **As a class**, read out a selection of alternative endings. Compare them with Leon Garfield's. Vote for the ones you judge to be as good, or better.

Then compile a class list headed **Ways of creating good endings to stories**. Draw ideas from your reading of other short stories as well as those you have just heard.

The Great Secret by **George H. Smith**

1 **In pairs**, act out a meeting between the DA and another of Maraat's victims after the story ends. Conversation turns to why Maraat is such a successful blackmailer. Talk about:

- the types of victim he chooses, and why
- his blackmailing technique
- his manner when the DA interviews him
- his eyes
- possible ways in which he might be caught.

Does the DA think Maraat is playing a clever con trick, or is he convinced that the man really *does* have unusual powers?

2 **As a class**, find evidence that *The Great Secret* could be described in both style and structure as:

- a detective story
- a thriller
- a science fiction story.

Your evidence can be 'for' or 'against'. Use what you know about the typical subject-matter and structure of these kinds of story to help you. Show what you think by filling in a grid, like this:

Detective story?		Thriller?		Science Fiction story?	
For	*Against*	*For*	*Against*	*For*	*Against*
1	1	1	1	1	1
2	2	2	2	2	2

On balance, what kind of story would *you* describe it as? Has it been well planned to hold your interest all the way through?

3 **By yourself**, imagine that you are Maraat.

After being released by the DA, you decide to celebrate by blackmailing a celebrity – someone well known to the public, e.g. a pop singer, a TV or film star, a famous sportsperson, a politician, a member of the Royal Family, etc. This time, however, your victim proves far less easy to hold to ransom.

Write the story of what happens. Tell it *either* from Maraat's viewpoint, using the first person *or* as a third-person narrative. Build up to a tense, exciting ending.

Pure Rotten by **John Lutz**

1 **In small groups**, exchange ideas about what is going on in this story. Say what you think about:

- the attitude of 'A. Snatcher' towards blackmailing Mr and Mrs Forthcue

- Mr Forthcue's replies to the blackmail letters, and what these show about him

- the letter Pure Rotten writes to her stepfather, and what this shows about her.

2 **As a class**, consider the form and structure the writer has chosen for this story: the transcript of a phone call, followed by 11 letters.

How well does the story's form suit its subject – particularly at the beginning and the end? In making your judgement, think how well *Pure Rotten* would work as:

- a conventional story, told in the third person

- a television play-script.

Draw up a chart to show the advantages and disadvantages of these two forms compared with that which the writer actually uses, like this:

Advantages and disadvantages of *Pure Rotten* in:		
Conventional story form	Television play-script form	Its actual form
1	1	1
2	2	2

3 **By yourself**, write Mr Forthcue's reply to the last letter from Snatchers, Inc., dated June 1.

What you make him say will depend on **(a)** what you think he'll work out from the letter of June 1, and **(b)** your idea of his feelings towards Pure Rotten.

His letter might contain a few surprises that give an extra twist to the story.

The First Day of School by **William Saroyan**

1   In small groups, exchange your own memories of
     starting school. What do you remember most? Why?
     What did you learn in the first few days?

     Compare your experience with Jim's. What will *he*
     remember most? Why? What does *he* learn?

2   The writer builds up this story by describing how Jim's
     feelings about school change as time goes on.

     In pairs, trace these changes in the form of a flow
     diagram, showing how the story's structure helps you
     understand Jim's reactions to starting school. Do it like
     this:

What Jim feels	Quotation to show this
He is frightened by the idea of starting school because it's completely new to him.	'Jim liked Amy, but he didn't like her for taking him to school.'
His fears are confirmed when he first goes inside the school building: it's very different from home, and he knows he'll soon be parted from Amy.	'The halls and rooms scared her, and him, and the smell of the place too.'

Make about *six* further entries. When you have finished,
look over your diagram and decide how far Jim has
'fitted in' at school by the end of the story.

Why do you think so much of the story is set out in
single lines?

3 **As a class**, consider why the relationship between Jim and Amy is important to this story.

Talk about:

- the part Amy has played in Jim's life before he starts school
- her feelings when she is walking him to school and when she meets the principal
- her feelings when she leaves him in the classroom, and on her way back home
- her feelings when she collects him at the end of his first day
- why 'for some reason tears came to her eyes' at the end of the story.

What is the *pattern* of change in Jim's relationship with Amy between the beginning and the end of the story? How does this run parallel to Jim's experience of school as he starts to settle in (see Activity 2)?

4 **By yourself**, write a story from the viewpoint of a child of five, or younger.

It need not be about a 'big event' such as starting school. Children are strongly affected by anything that is new to them, however ordinary it seems to older people.

Choose a style and structure suited to your subject. You could write a first-person narrative *or* write in the third person from a first-person point of view (as in *The First Day of School*).

Sing-Song Time by **Joyce Grenfell**

1 **In pairs**, choose two extracts from *Sing-Song Time* you particularly like. Each should be about 20 lines long.

Take one extract each. Perform it to your partner, using the Infant School teacher's tone of voice (notice how this keeps changing), suitable actions and gestures, and pauses at appropriate points.

Do you think Joyce Grenfell captures accurately the way teachers talk to young children? To help you decide, recall how your own teachers spoke to the class when you were between four and six.

2 *Sing-Song Time* is a story built on a conversation where only one person is heard speaking. Its structure invites you to mentally 'fill in the gaps' as you read.

In small groups, try doing this on paper. Some gaps will be filled in by the children's comments, others by descriptions of what's happening in the classroom. For example:

> **Kenny, why haven't you taken your coat off?**
> *Miss, my mummy says I've to put my coat on when I go out, so I'm keeping it on, miss, 'cos it's wet and cold and rainy, miss, and I've got to go for my tea, and . . .*
> **No, it isn't time to go home yet, Kenny! You've only just come.**
> [Kenny starts to walk towards the door, still in his coat. Sidney punches him as he passes. Kenny begins to cry.]
> **Kenny, you've only been here about ten minutes. Come and sit on the floor next to Susan.**

Choose at least two sections of the story, each about 10 lines long. Make the children speak more than just a few words.

Then join up **with another group**. Take turns to perform what you have written. How realistic do you judge the writing to be? Award each other marks out of ten to show what you think.

3 **By yourself**, write a story which has the same form and structure as *Sing-Song Time*. Choose your own situation and setting OR use one of the following:

- a harassed parent at a three-year-old's birthday party

- a teacher leading a group of teenage pupils on a trip to the zoo OR a historic building OR the Millennium Dome, etc.

- an aerobics instructor taking a class of physically unfit people.

Love Letters by **Kate Walker**

1 **In small groups**, count up the number of letters in this story. Would it be true to describe it as a 'letters story' (cf. *Pure Rotten*, page 13)?

Look at the extract from Clive's letter to Helen on pages 30 and 31. How would you describe its style? Why do you think Clive writes to his girlfriend in this way?

Clive's letter comes right in the *middle* of the story. Show how it acts as the turning-point in *Love Letters* by considering:

- the effect it has on Nick

- why it leads to him writing his last letter to Fleur, telling her 'I think we should call it off'.

2 **As a class**, look again at the opening paragraph of the story. It is written by Nick, in the first person. Try rewriting it in the *third person*, using the past tense.

Compare the two versions. Why do you think the writer has chosen to present the story through Nick's eyes and in his voice? How do (**a**) the style, and (**b**) the structure of *Love Letters* reflect Nick's viewpoint?

3 **In pairs**, share the writing of a story made up partly, or entirely, of letters. Use or include e-mails if you wish.

Choose your own subject. Some possibilities are:

- a story about boy-girl relationships
- The Crime That Went Horribly Wrong
- The Computers Write Back
- Correspondence from the Past OR Future.

Plan your story carefully. Make sure it has a strong enough plot to hold your reader's interest to the end. If possible, do it on a computer so that you can create different formats, as well as different writing styles.

Romantic Interlude by **Timothy Callender**

1   **In small groups,** find up to *five* examples of Big Joe's talent for getting into trouble or having accidents.

As you talk, fill in a chart like this:

Big Joe in trouble		
Event	**Setting**	**Cause**
1 BJ robbed of his money and clothes by two strangers	the local pub	BJ allows the strangers to get him drunk after he's been dumped by Sheila
2		

Take *one* episode you have listed. Build up and perform a drama sketch around it. Base it on the details in the story. You can add further dialogue and characters to make it more amusing/farcical.

2   **In pairs,** choose a passage you particularly enjoy. It should run to between 1 and 1½ pages.

Divide it up between you, then (after practising) read it aloud to another pair. Bring out: the narrator's *tone of voice*; the speech style of the characters; the *pace* and *rhythm* of the narrative; the humour.

Take turns with your listeners to make a verbal assessment of how well you have brought the story to life.

3   *Romantic Interlude* is a 'spoken story'. Its main purpose is to entertain.

As a class, look at the ways in which its style and structure are *anecdotal* – as if the narrator is speaking to a small group of friends in Barbados.

Find examples of how the narrator:

- uses a conversational (or 'colloquial') story-telling style

- uses a sequence of fast-moving *episode*s to carry the story forward, as in a film

- begins paragraphs and leads from one paragraph to the next

- builds up suspense.

Now choose three sentences from the story where (**a**) the vocabulary, and (**b**) the grammar differ from Standard English. Re-write them in a standard form. What do you think has been lost?

Do you think the story works well – or is it too 'over the top' to be effective?

4   By yourself, write a 'tall story' in an anecdotal style.

If you wish, use the dialect of your own (or any other) part of the country. Draw on some of the story-telling techniques you have examined in *Romantic Interlude*.

You could make a tape-recording of your finished version for others to listen to rather than read.

Like Mother, Like Son by **Pauline Cartledge**

1 **In pairs**, say what you think the story shows about:

- the relationship between mother and son in 1955

- the relationship between mother and son in 1997

- how mother and son are alike.

What else could this 50-word story be said to be about? Boarding schools? Homes for the elderly? How families treat their ageing parents? Revenge?

How does its 'four letters' structure reflect its theme?

2 **As a class**, share your reactions to this story – and to the mini-saga *form*.

A short story normally has (**a**) a plot, (**b**) at least two characters, (**c**) a setting, or settings, and (**d**) a theme, or themes. How many of these elements are present in *Like Mother, Like Son*? If the answer is 'all of them', are you surprised?

Talk about some ways in which you might construct your *own* mini-saga. You could, for example, try:

- an exchange of notes, faxes, memos, etc.

- doodles on the cover of an exercise book, inside a school text book, or on a desk

- a 'silent' conversation between people thinking their own thoughts

- a narrative made up of 50 one-word sentences

. . . and so on.

3 **By yourself**, draft and write your own mini-saga.

If possible, do it on screen so that you can: re-write; re-arrange text; experiment with word patterns; use different layouts and fonts, etc.

Remember to use exactly 50 words, excluding the title.

4 *Like Mother, Like Son* won first prize in a Mini-Saga Competition run by a national newspaper. There were over 7,000 entries. Some were Runners-Up, others were Highly Commended.

As a class, hold a similar competition for your finished mini-sagas. Everyone should take part in the judging – and be prepared to justify their opinions.

A Cautionary Tale in mini-saga form

Perhaps There's Something to be Said for the Three Rs After All

by Nicholas Hodgson

At school he had been no good at maths but outstanding at writing and reading. But who needs arithmetic?

He entered the competition with enthusiasm and produced a dazzling, witty, profound and paradoxical story. He was inspired. It was an absolute masterpiece.

The judges sighed. Another one with 51 words.

Saturday the Fifth by **Kate Edwards**

1 **In small groups**, exchange ideas about exactly what happened at 16 Jeremiah Avenue on Saturday 5th September. Say who you think was involved, and why.

You may come up with different ideas. If so, explain your reasoning to other group members. Refer to earlier parts of the story to support your views.

2 **By yourself**, write a description of the events at Ray Jennings's house on 5th September.

Use *one* of the following forms:

- a short story written in the third person

- an eye-witness account given by Maxine Walker

- a police report filed by Sergeant Johnson about what he found at the house *and* the results of the enquiry that followed.

Write in a style suited to the form you choose.

3 **As a class**, look closely at the letters written by the people listed below. How much can you tell about them from (**a**) what they say, and (**b**) the way they set out and write their letters? Note your answers on a chart like this:

Character points			
Maxine Walker	**Wendy Short**	**Karen Parker**	**Stephen Haley**
1	1	1	1
2	2	2	2

Concentrate on (**a**) the sort of people they seem to be, and (**b**) their purpose in writing to the paper.

4 **As a class**, consider whether the writer intends *Saturday the Fifth* to be chiefly:

- a crime story

- a mystery story

- a story about animal rights.

Use your knowledge of some typical structures of these types of story to help you decide. For example:

- a crime story often builds up questions in your mind about 'whodunnit?' or 'howdunnit?'

- a mystery story often leaves you uncertain about the cause of events

- an animal rights story might feature an animal as the central character and divide the humans into 'goodies' and 'baddies'.

Then discuss ideas for a story of your own made up entirely of extracts from a newspaper, or newspapers. **By yourself**, write the story.

The Dead Don't Steal by **Ella Griffiths**

1   **In pairs**, write a front-page story for *The Norwegian Daily Star* with the headline:

> **BERGEN SECRETARY'S KILLER CAUGHT!**
>
> **'Daring' police tactics pay off**

Reconstruct for your readers the story of how the police drew Curt into their net. Include only *essential* details. If possible do this on a computer.

2   **As a class**, look carefully at the way this story makes use of a lengthy *flashback* sequence as part of its structure. It runs from 'Everything had gone so well . . .' (page 52) to 'It was beginning to seem unreal' (page 54).

Consider the following:

- The writer could have *begun* her story by describing these events. Why do you think she chose not to?

- Are these events strictly necessary to the plot of the story? Give reasons for your view.

3   **In small groups**, re-read the story's final section on page 58. One reader has commented: 'The ending seems hugely predictable'. Do you agree?

To help you decide, ask yourselves:

- Did you realise that Inspector Svendsen was bluffing Curt all through the story?

- Did you guess that the police operation must have involved a woman who looked like Lill?

- Did you predict that Curt would be pressured into returning to where he had hidden Lill's body?

Look back through the text for evidence to support what you say.

On balance, do you think the structure of *The Dead Don't Steal* helps to create an effective ending?

4   **By yourself**, make up a story which includes one or more flashback sequences. Choose your own subject. It can be a crime story if you wish.

At the end, write a short account of the effects you were trying to achieve by using flashback. Say whether or not you are pleased with the result, and why.

A *Pound of Flesh* by **Kristin Silva**

1   In pairs, act out a conversation in the hospital where this story ends between *either* the girl's parents *or* one parent and the girl's doctor.

Bring out: what happened to the girl, and why; her parents' emotions; the outlook for the future.

2 In form, *A Pound of Flesh* is a 'collage story'.

As a class, talk about (**a**) how it has been put together, and (**b**) why it is set out as it is. Identify its various strands by finding examples of the following:

Magazine/ newspaper cuttings and quotes	Extracts from advertise- ments	The writer's own comments	The girl's narrative
1	1	1	1
2	2	2	2

Why do you think the writer chooses to print the girl's narrative side by side with passages of non-fiction? How does this structure help convey the story's theme?

3   In small groups, look closely at the style and structure of the passage on page 65 beginning 'Stupid' and ending:

'. . . A blur fuzzy at the edges. Focusing.'

What do you learn from this passage about the girl's feelings towards (**a**) other people, including her family, and (**b**) herself? How does the way it is set out reflect these feelings?

If the passage had been written in conventional sentences and paragraphs, would it carry the same force?

4 **By yourself**, write a collage story on a subject likely to be of importance to teenagers in general, as well as of interest to you.

One way of planning and drafting is as follows:

- over several weeks, save cuttings from newspapers and magazines on your chosen theme

- develop a fictional narrative around the cuttings you collect

- find further material from books, brochures, web-sites etc. which you may be able to use

- on a computer, try out cut-and-paste techniques to achieve a form that matches the purpose of your writing.

Forbidden Clothes by **Jamila Gavin**

1   This story is structured in episodes, rather like the scenes in a television play. There are ten in all. Each is marked by a gap in the text.

In pairs, look back at each episode and give it a brief heading to summarise what it describes.

Then, **as a class**, compare the headings you've come up with. Justify your choices by referring to the text.

Talk about which episodes are based on *conflicts.* What causes these? Which episode do you think is the most important one in the story as a whole?

2   **By yourself**, imagine you are Nasreen *before* she moves out to live with the Dibbens.

Write three entries in her diary. They describe:

1 *A typical day in her life before she makes friends with Louise*	2 *The evening of the day she meets Carl*	3 *The day she decides to leave home* ....

Base what you write on the details in the story. Bring out Nasreen's changing feelings as time goes on, using a suitable writing style.

3   By short-story standards, there are a lot of characters in *Forbidden Clothes.*

As a class, decide whether the following are 'major' or 'minor' characters:

- Margot Henderson
- Louise's brother, Craig
- Nasreen's head teacher
- Mrs Khan
- Carl
- Louise
- Mr Khan

Then take each character you consider to be a 'major' one. Draw up a class chart to show what part they play in the structure of the story as a whole.

Rendezvous by **Daniel Ransom**

1 **In pairs**, draw a diagram of the story's plot-line, showing how Payton and Kim come to make their 'rendezvous'. Do it like this:

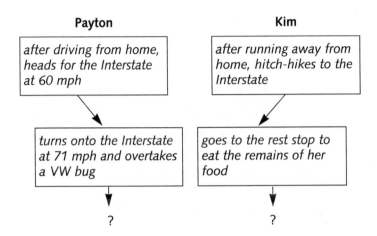

Payton

> after driving from home, heads for the Interstate at 60 mph

> turns onto the Interstate at 71 mph and overtakes a VW bug

?

Kim

> after running away from home, hitch-hikes to the Interstate

> goes to the rest stop to eat the remains of her food

?

Study your completed diagram. Does it reveal any *patterns*? Why do you think the writer has chosen a 'journey' structure for this story?

2 **In pairs**, note down all the references to Payton's and Kim's lives in the recent past. Say what these tell you about their relationships with others.

Then act out both the following conversations:

a) Payton confessing to the priest before he drives to the Interstate

b) Kim talking to her mother before she runs away from home.

Do you see any similarities in character between Payton and Kim?

3 **In small groups,** look closely at the second 'Payton' section and the second 'Kim' section. Pick out from each:

- a sentence written in the third person and the present tense

- a sentence written from each character's viewpoint, explaining something about their feelings

- a sentence written in the voice of the two characters concerned, to show them thinking aloud

- a deliberately ungrammatical sentence.

Then, **as a class**, say what you think the writer tries to achieve by using this *mixture* of styles. Does the way this story is set out, almost like a list, make it seem disjointed – or does it help the writer achieve his purpose, as you understand it?

4 **By yourself,** write a story on a theme of your own entitled *Rendezvous*.

It will be about two characters meeting, for whatever reason, and should use the same 'sectional' form as *Rendezvous*. Whether the characters already know each other is for you to decide – as is the kind of *ending* you write. Will you leave the outcome of the meeting uncertain, as in Daniel Ransom's story?

Dog on Board by **Dennis Hamley**

1   Divide your class into Team 1 and Team 2.

a) Team 1 notes down *in order* what happens to Amy's family, from when she has her nightmare to the point where Dad stops at the red light on page 94.

b) Team 2 notes down *in order* what happens to the two lorry drivers, from when Arthur Rowntree drives into fog on the M4 to the point where the Cornishman reaches the top of the hill on page 94.

Make your notes in the form of flow-diagrams.

Then, **as a class**, compare notes. Discuss:

- what they show about the *time-scale* of events: why is this unusual?

- what is meant by the term *parallel plot*: how does the writer make use of this device?

- the story's *ending*: whereabouts do you think it occurs?

2   **In pairs**, imagine the events that take place immediately after the story stops.

Write and present a news report for Radio Cornwall about what happens on the road leading to the camp site. You could include several interviews – with Arthur Rowntree? with a local resident who was an eye-witness? with the owner of Trelawney's Transport?

If possible, tape-record your report.

3   **In small groups**, note down all the references you can find to the dog, Goldie. Do it like this:

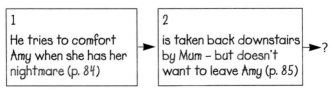

. . . and so on.

Join up with another group. Compare your findings. Why is Goldie important to the structure of the story as a whole?

4 By yourself, imagine you are the Cornish driver.

Write an account of your day's journey, using the first person and *either* the past tense *or* a combination of past and present tenses. Take some details from the story; invent others yourself.

Include your *thoughts* and *feelings* at different points during the journey – particularly at the end.

The Gulf by **Geraldine McCaughrean**

1   **In small groups**, say what you know by the end of the story about its plot, its characters and its setting.

Discuss the following questions:

- Who is Juan? what is he fleeing from? why?

- What, and where, is 'the gulf'?

- Who are the people across the gulf – the sisters, the brothers, the mothers, the old people, Father?

- What is the story's central event?

Why do you think the writer does not provide precise answers to some of these questions? Does this spoil the story for you?

2   **As a class,** think about some typical features of *fable* and *myth*.

Begin by pooling your memories of Aesop's fable *The Tortoise and the Hare.* What happens in it, exactly? What moral or 'message' does it have?

Talk about other fables and myths you know.

- What sort of things happen in them?

- What drives the narrative?

- What are the characters like?

- Where is the action set?

Then compare *The Gulf* with these types of story. Draw up a class chart to show the similarities and differences, like this:

Elements similar to those in fable and myth	Elements different from those in fable and myth
1	1
2	2

The Gulf was written in 1999. Why do you think the writer chose the form she did for a contemporary story?

3 **In pairs**, re-read the first two paragraphs and the last two paragraphs of *The Gulf*.

Make a chart to show how paragraphs 1 and 2 create the feeling that Juan is in great danger. Do it like this:

Textual detail	Impression it gives
'He ran until every searchlight, floodlight and white-winking barrack window was out of sight . . .'	J. is being hunted by the 'authorities', who are powerful and well-equipped to catch people who escape (across a military border?) – by contrast, J. is alone and unsure of his bearings
'No one ever did, they had told him. No one ever would'	The odds are stacked against J. – the repetition of 'No one' emphasises this

Now make a similar chart to show how the last two paragraphs give the feeling that, in crossing the gulf, Juan will achieve a new and happier life.

Compare your two grids. What do they show about the *pattern* of the story as a whole? How does this structure reflect the main themes of *The Gulf*?

4 **By yourself**, choose a theme for a story which you consider to be 'timeless'.

Develop a story around this theme. Then write it in the form of a fable. Make use of some of the writing techniques you have examined in *The Gulf*.

Using the Collection

The chart opposite has been created to help teachers make full and flexible use of the stories in this book.

For more information and suggestions on using the collection, please see p. vii.

Title	Theme/Genre	Main features of form/structure	Particularly striking opening	Particularly striking ending
Voodoo (page 1)	Crime	Twist ending: third-person voice		✓
A Grave Misunderstanding (page 3)	Supernatural (comic)	Animal viewpoint: first-person voice	✓	
The Great Secret (page 9)	Crime thriller	Twist ending: third-person voice		✓
Pure Rotten (page 13)	Crime thriller	Letters narrative: first-person voices	✓	✓
The First Day of School (page 18)	School/Childhood	Third-person voice, first-person viewpoint		✓
Sing-Song Time (page 24)	School/Childhood	Monologue: first-person voice	✓	
Love Letters (page 28)	Teenage boy-girl relationship	First-person voice and viewpoint	✓	
Romantic Interlude (page 33)	Teenage boy-girl relationship (comic)	Spoken story: third-person voice, first-person viewpoint		✓
Like Mother, Like Son (page 41)	Generations	Mini-saga, letters format: first-person voices		✓
Saturday the Fifth (page 42)	Murder mystery	Letters narrative, newspaper items: first- and third-person voices and viewpoints		✓
The Dead Don't Steal (page 50)	Murder mystery	Twist ending, use of flashback sequences: third-person voice, first-person viewpoint	✓	✓
A Pound of Flesh (page 59)	Social-cultural pressures on adolescent	Collage story: mix of fiction (first-person voice) and factual items (third-person voice)	✓	✓
Forbidden Clothes (page 67)	Social-cultural pressures on adolescents	Linked episodes, filmic structure: third-person voice		✓
Rendezvous (page 80)	Teenage rebellion	Dual narrative, journey structure: third-person voice, first-person viewpoints	✓	
Dog on Board (page 84)	Supernatural/Real	Dual perspective/parallel plots, journey structure: third-person voice, first-person viewpoints		✓
The Gulf (page 95)	Supernatural/Real	Fable/allegory: third-person voice, first-person viewpoint	✓	

Heinemann
New Windmills

Founding Editors: Anne and Ian Serraillier

Chinua Achebe Things Fall Apart
David Almond Skellig
Maya Angelou I Know Why the Caged Bird Sings
Margaret Atwood The Handmaid's Tale
Jane Austen Pride and Prejudice
J G Ballard Empire of the Sun
Stan Barstow Joby; A Kind of Loving
Nina Bawden Carrie's War; Devil by the Sea; Kept in the Dark; The Finding; Humbug
Lesley Beake A Cageful of Butterflies
Malorie Blackman Tell Me No Lies; Words Last Forever
Ray Bradbury The Golden Apples of the Sun; The Illustrated Man
Betsy Byars The Midnight Fox; The Pinballs; The Not-Just-Anybody Family; The Eighteenth Emergency
Victor Canning The Runaways
Jane Leslie Conly Racso and the Rats of NIMH
Susan Cooper King of Shadows
Robert Cormier We All Fall Down; Heroes
Roald Dahl Danny, The Champion of the World; The Wonderful Story of Henry Sugar; George's Marvellous Medicine; The BFG; The Witches; Boy; Going Solo; Matilda; My Year
Anita Desai The Village by the Sea
Charles Dickens A Christmas Carol; Great Expectations; Hard Times; Oliver Twist; A Charles Dickens Selection
Berlie Doherty Granny was a Buffer Girl; Street Child
Roddy Doyle Paddy Clarke Ha Ha Ha
Anne Fine The Granny Project
Jamila Gavin The Wheel of Surya
Graham Greene The Third Man and The Fallen Idol; Brighton Rock
Thomas Hardy The Withered Arm and Other Wessex Tales
L P Hartley The Go-Between
Ernest Hemmingway The Old Man and the Sea; A Farewell to Arms
Barry Hines A Kestrel For A Knave
Nigel Hinton Getting Free; Buddy; Buddy's Song; Out of the Darkness
Anne Holm I Am David
Janni Howker Badger on the Barge; The Nature of the Beast; Martin Farrell

Pete Johnson The Protectors
Jennifer Johnston Shadows on Our Skin
Geraldine Kaye Comfort Herself
Daniel Keyes Flowers for Algernon
Dick King-Smith The Sheep-Pig
Elizabeth Laird Red Sky in the Morning; Kiss the Dust
D H Lawrence The Fox and The Virgin and the Gypsy; Selected Tales
George Layton The Swap
Harper Lee To Kill a Mockingbird
C Day Lewis The Otterbury Incident
Joan Lingard Across the Barricades; The File on Fraulein Berg
Penelope Lively The Ghost of Thomas Kempe
Jack London The Call of the Wild; White Fang
Bernard MacLaverty Cal; The Best of Bernard Mac Laverty
James Vance Marshall Walkabout
Ian McEwan The Daydreamer; A Child in Time
Michael Morpurgo My Friend Walter; The Wreck of the Zanzibar;
The War of Jenkins' Ear; Why the Whales Came; Arthur, High King
of Britain; Kensuke's Kingdom; Hereabout Hill
Beverley Naidoo No Turning Back
Bill Naughton The Goalkeeper's Revenge
New Windmill A Charles Dickens Selection
New Windmill Book of Classic Short Stories
New Windmill Book of Fiction and Non-fiction: Taking Off!
New Windmill Book of Haunting Tales
New Windmill Book of Humorous Stories: Don't Make Me Laugh
New Windmill Book of Nineteenth Century Short Stories
New Windmill Book of Non-fiction: Get Real!
New Windmill Book of Non-fiction: Real Lives, Real Times
New Windmill Book of Scottish Short Stories
New Windmill Book of Short Stories: Fast and Curious
New Windmill Book of Short Stories: From Beginning to End
New Windmill Book of Short Stories: Into the Unknown
New Windmill Book of Short Stories: Tales with a Twist
New Windmill Book of Short Stories: Trouble in Two Centuries
New Windmill Book of Short Stories: Ways with Words
New Windmill Book of Short Stories by Women
New Windmill Book of Stories from many Cultures and Traditions:
Fifty-Fifty Tutti-Frutti Chocolate-Chip
New Windmill Book of Stories from Many Genres: Myths, Murders
and Mysteries

How many have you read?